Little Jamaica

WATERBUCK
www.water-buck.co.uk

WATERBUCK PUBLISHING LIMITED
LONDON, UK

First published in Great Britain in 2008
by WATERBUCK PUBLISHING

ISBN 0 9548630 1 1

Executive Editor: Nicholas Harrison
Chief Editor: Anthony Murphy
Editor: George Kelly

Typesetting: Waterbuck Publishing
Photography: tony.murphy@hotmail.co.uk
All rights reserved.

WATERBUCK PUBLISHING LIMITED
Waterbuck House, Office 125,
14 Tottenham Court Road
London W1T 1JY

WWW.WATERBUCK.CO.UK

CAUTION!

This piece of literature is written in:
Jamaican Patois
UK Street Slang
English Arabic

If you are unfamiliar with any words or phrases, please refer to the glossary at the back.

Little Jamaica

Dedicated to all the
Poverty Driven Children
that lost their lives on the streets

Change the way we think...

Peace,

Von "Nicke Nicks" Mozar

R.I.P (Rise. In. Peace)
My Granddad - Da'son
My Grandmothers - Ma'Pums and Mudda Murph'
My Little Brother - Christopher Jerome Harrison

PART ONE

Late 1940s:
Somewhere In The
Atlantic Ocean

Chapter One

'Mi seh mi ah bad man!'

'Da'son, no!'

Da'son's wife pulls away his huge shovel-like hand from the white man's face, which has turned red from fear.

Da'son's little daughter grabs his leg and begins to cry. 'Daddy no, please, Daddy no.'

Da'son looks down at his daughter; his rage settles instantly. He cuts his eye at the white man, kisses his teeth, then leads his daughter and wife away.

The spectators who witness the ending of the armshouse whisper amongst each other as Da'son walks past them with his family.

'You see, that's why white people think that we are all animals, because of ignorant black people like him.'

'True, true.'

Da'son hears the whispers and feels to explain why the armshouse began but cannot be bothered. He knows that these nose-in-the-air posh Jamaicans still wouldn't care that this white man—who had too much to drink—shouted at his daughter, made her cry, and almost pushed her on the floor.

Da'son approaches the white man and, using his best Queen's English, and in a very respectful tone, says, 'Excuse me, sir, what me daughter do to make you shout at her and almost push her on the floor?'

The white man replies with a drunken stutter. 'Well, you should know...sir...that your kind should not be allowed in certain parts of the ship.'

As the white man ends his sentence he waves his finger towards Da'son's daughter, and Da'son's eyes fill with rage. He responds in his patois, not caring if the white man understands or not. 'Ah weh yuh ah tark seh, fi mi kind?'

The white man obviously doesn't understand Da'son's thick Jamaican accent. 'Your kind, sir,' he slurs. 'Negros. Niggers.'

A large vein pulses out of Da'son's neck; his nose flares. No-one on his little island of Jamaica has ever called him a Negro or nigger and he takes this as a big disrespect. Exploding with rage, Da'son grabs the white man by his wrist and says, 'Hey dutty johncrow, mine how yuh ah tark. Mi wi lick down yuh blood-claat.'

The white man tries to pull away his arm, but Da'son has it gripped tighter than a vice. The fear seems to have sobered the white man a little; no more slurring. 'You don't scare me, you know. I can get the captain to arrest you and lock you down under the decks.'

Da'son lets go of the white man's wrist, then points his finger towards him. 'Yuh feel seh mi business?'

Da'son kisses his teeth. 'Mi ah bad man, nah mi ah di baddest man.'

The white man looks Da'son up and down like he's worthless. 'Oh, shut up you ignoramus,' he says, contempt in his voice. 'You don't know what it means to be a bad man. Let's just see how bad you are when you're refused entry into England. You do know that the British government are not going to let not even one of you primitive blacks into my beloved country?' The white man stumbles back slightly, and points his crooked finger. 'No niggers!'

Da'son's eyes widen. He rolls his fist into a ball to knock the white man out, show him that he doesn't care.

He raises his bulging fist and shouts, 'Mi seh mi ah bad man!'

Twelve Years Later

Chapter Two

Although some members of the government had wanted the ship to turn back around, along with any other black people that had made it into England previously, they were overruled. Probably by the members of the government whose forefathers were black slaves who had children with a white "English Rose".

Da'son made it off the ship and into the murky, chimney-smoke filled streets of Brixton, South London. Since then, Da'son has not encountered any racism directly; maybe this is due to his six-foot-six frame, or maybe due to his lack of interest in going down to the pub, which never allows in blacks, dogs or the Irish. This racial discrimination has prompted underground pubs, where black people or even the Irish can come and drink after a hard day's work building back up England's infrastructure.

Da'son has always thought that those same politicians who had wanted the ship to turn back around can probably no longer stand seeing more black people coming to England and having "fun". They have to stop these underground pubs and evict every last black person from the country. He also thinks that maybe the same politicians are also the ones that deployed the Teddy Boys to attack every black person that they saw on the streets of London. But after another weekend of attacks on black people, things are about to change...

A group of young black men coming from an underground pub are in conversation outside a house of a Teddy Boy. Their talking apparently wakes up the Teddy Boy's newborn baby.

The Teddy Boy flings open his window and starts to shout with asperity. 'Don't you know we'll kill all blacks? Down with niggers! Keep Britain white! Find a banana boat and go back to where you come from! You bunch of monkeys...'

The youngest member of the group smiles cockily and wonders: *why do so-called conscious beings still separate themselves into races? When it is evident that humans have surpassed nature mentally and therefore should not be looking at each other as black or white but as conscious beings.*

He rubs his nose and says, 'Rest yourself, man. We belong 'ere, dis is 'r country now.'

The Teddy Boy almost explodes at hearing a black man claiming his beloved England is his home. He slams his window shut and watches as the group of black men cross over the road to the bus stop. The other black men leave the youngest member by himself. The Teddy Boy looks at his watch, realising that the last bus has long gone and there would be no way a black cab would be picking up a black man in the black night. The Teddy Boy calls up his friends and tells them about the vile words that he had to endure from, how he saw it, the lowest form of life: a black man. The friends do not have to hear anymore; they reach the bus stop minutes later and give the young black boy the beating of his life. If they had brought a rope they would have lynched him.

After the Government and Police overlooked this brutal attack, the Teddy Boys had the rationale to support their terror campaign under the guise of stopping these "troublesome" underground pubs. Things got so bad that black people were afraid to leave their homes after dark; so then mobs of racist white people began attacking black people's homes, too. It got so bad some black people contemplated going back to their country. But then one evening a young black man was chased by a group of Teddy Boys, and if not for the protection from a white shop owner the Teddy Boys would have killed him. If this had happened, the streets of London would have suffered ten times the violence because that young black boy was, and is, Da'son's brother in-law.

Da'son's wife runs into the sitting room crying, telling him about what had just happened to her brother. Da'son squints his eyes. The imprint of his jawline shows through his skin. He slams down his paper, then picks up his phone and dials.

Chapter Three

It isn't hard for Da'son to rally up a group of men; he has a natural persuasive way about him that could influence even the most closed-minded people to take action.

Da'son's large dining room, which smells of fried fish and peppered onions, is packed full of serious-faced hardworking black men. Da'son stands up to get the mens' attention. Everyone falls quiet.

'Yeah, mi tank everybady who deah yah tinite.' Da'son pauses as if to collect his thoughts. He clears his throat. 'Everybady si di problem dem whey wi a face, but mi nuh sure if unnu si di real libaty whey a gwan?' Da'son laughs without humour and licks his lips. 'Unnu waah know di real libaty? Figet bout whey di politician bwoy a mek di racist bwoy get whey wid.' Da'son hammers his fist on the table. 'Caah dem a tek wi fi slave.' Da'son pauses again, letting the word "slave" penetrate the minds of the men. 'Dat a di libaty. Memba,' he says, 'dem invite wi to dem country wid false pramise, den di racists politician bwoy a campaign fi send wi back a wi yawd wid wi shut button, after wi help dem fight dem war an den help build up back dem country. A suh dem treat wi? Jus lackka how dem treat fi-wi African ancesta dem fram inna di 1500s straight up to inna di 1800s when dem bring thousand a dem yah suh and wuk dem like dawg.' Da'son points his large sausage-like finger. 'Unnu ah hear mi?'

The group of men reply with grunts and groans.

'Mi a tell yuh a slavery ting dis.' Da'son laughs cynically. 'Dem ah tek wi fi fool, dem waan di Teddy Bwoy dem fi run us back ah yawd. Dat's why dem nah duh nuttun bout dem.' Da'son kisses his teeth, leans forward with his fist on the oak table, and in a low tone says, 'Mi nuh know bout unnu, but yuh see mi, mi naah left yah suh wid out a house. Yuh tink seh me ah bruk my back ah wuk seven dayz a week fi nuttun, no sah, nuttun nuh guh suh, book nuh read suh.'

The group respond in unison. 'Yeah man, yeah man.'

'Memba wi nuh slave,' Da'son continues. 'Memba wi have wi right fi live anywhey inna Hingland. And mek mi tell yuh dis, mi nuh fraid fi dead inna Landan tinite. Mi a tell yuh di great leadda Marcus Garvey dead right yah suh inna Landan, suh wi nuh fi fraid an mek dem run wi fram bout yah. Wi fi show dem seh, dem cyaan tek nuh more libaty wid wi.'

Da'son hammers his fist again on the table. 'Mek dem know seh wi a BAD MAN!'

At this moment Da'son's five year old son who is hiding and listening to his father's war speech, feels the hairs on the back of his neck stand up.

Da'son's son quickly runs out of his hiding space as his dad and the group of men take to the night streets in preparation for an epic battle.

A battle for respect.

Chapter Four

Da'son's son sneaks into the boot of his car. Without noticing, Da'son jumps in and drives off to find some Teddy Boys. It isn't long before he finds some.

At first the Teddy Boys don't know what to make of Da'son pulling up his car opposite them and just staring.

Da'son and three other men step out of the car.

The Teddy Boys, who are all wearing a velvet collar and cuff long jacket with drain-pipe trousers, look at each other in amazement. Then, the one who seems to be the leader runs his hand through his greased-up long hair. 'If you know what's good for you wogs,' he says, 'you'll get back in your car and piss off!'

Da'son and the others show no reaction.

The leader shouts: 'You hear me? Hey! I said piss off, before we have your guts for garters.'

Four cars come zooming out from a couple of side streets. The doors shoot open. Serious-face black men step out. The Teddy Boys freeze with fear; they have no time to flick out their butterfly knives as black fists hit them from every angle.

Da'son's son pushes down the back seat, just in time to see his dad knocking out a Teddy Boy cold. The Teddy Boy hits the ground and the impact splits his skull open. Blood runs from the wound. Da'son's son looks on in excitement, which then turns to fear as a pub door busts open and a group of shouting, weapon-wielding, Teddy Boys come charging out.

Da'son and his men stand firm; they're even able to disarm some of the crazy Teddy Boys but the pressure is too much. Half of Da'son's men are now twisted on the floor. It seems Da'son and his men will be defeated.

On seeing this, Da'son's son has the urge to jump out of the car to help, but backup appears from an underground black pub, where the Teddy Boys had been waiting earlier to beat up some black men, whom they call "Wogs".

The battle has evened up, in numbers at least but not in determination; the Teddy Boys are getting their heads cracked open by bricks, bottles and black fists.

Some white women come out of the pub screaming and begging for the violence to end. The Teddy Boys feel that they've lost the battle and know these black men mean business—they aren't going to stop battling. So one by one the Teddy Boys retreat, limping away bloodied and in pain, leaving behind strong black men who stand proud.

The black men can't stand for long lapping up their victory as police sirens can be heard coming from afar. In less than a minute the street is cleared of black men and all that is left is the evidence of no more BS.

Chapter Five

The atmosphere inside Da'son's dining room has changed from two hours ago. It now has a vibe of a party; these black men have something to celebrate. They have won the "first battle" while showing they would not be intimidated and scared out of a country that they have every right to be in, and live in, without fear of attacks.

Da'son enters his dining room with his fist wrapped in bandage, holding a beer. Everyone falls silent.

'Yes, mi breddrins,' he says. 'Mi love how unnu stand up and fight dung dem racist white bwoy.'

'Cool nuh man, jus cool man,' echoes the room.

Da'son puts down his beer and raises his chin. 'Dis day here,' he begins in his best English accent, which he uses to talk among his white colleagues. 'Mark dis day—' Da'son uses his finger to make a cross on the wall. 'Dis day may go down in forgotten history but will live on inside every new generation after we. Yes, it will live on and protect da new generation from any liberties because dey will know dey have da right to stand up and fight.'

Tables and doors are banged in salute to Da'son's words. Da'son continues in patios. 'Unnu ah hear mi?' He smiles. 'Yeah, man, da next generation will know dey have a right to be in dis country, dey will know they're worth something and if any white racist bwoy test, dat get lick down.'

The room is filled with a symphony of noise. Da'son raises his voice above it. 'A'rite me breddrins, drink up and merry, memba wi win dis battle so all wi af fi do now is win dis war.'

Da'son picks up his beer and spots his son by the open door, and with only eye contact sends him to bed. Slowly Da'son's son moves away from the door, taking with him a mentality that could either turn him into a great conscious being or a notorious bad man.

The music is turned up, getting the party on its way. More beer flows as dominos are flung down onto tables. And laughter, with a concession of Ska tunes, are heard into the wee hours of the morning.

Late 1970's

Chapter Six

Railton Road—"The Frontline"—is an adjoining road that connects Brixton to Herne Hill and it's an area thriving with a new generation of two groups of racist individuals who call themselves Skin Heads and Mods. They are modern day Teddy Boys, with steel capped boots and three buttoned suits.

A gang of Skin Heads almost stabbed to death one of Da'son's son's school friends. Da'son's son, who he named Nattielous but who ended up being called Natty-Nya because of his I-don't-care attitude, is now eighteen years old. Him and the rest of his friends (who later will be known as the Raiders Posse following the '81 Brixton riots) are planning to unleash a violent bloody revenge upon the Skin Heads.

Natty-Nya runs down the creaking staircase in his neatly pressed flares with a blue beret on top of his trimmed afro, which will soon become dreadlocks.

'Yes, Granny?' he says in a gentle tone as he steps through the door and into the mothball-smelling sitting room.

'Yuh neva hear mi a call yuh, bwoy?'

'No, Granny,' replies Natty-Nya as he looks at his granny's ash black, wise old face and beautiful broad fat nose.

'Yuh sweep dung di stairs an tidy yuh room yet?'

Natty-Nya looks towards the floor. 'Yes, Granny.'

'A'rite, come gi mi some ice wata.'

Natty-Nya picks up the see-through plastic cup that his granny used her lips to point at and leaves the room. He returns with ice water. Before he can put the cup back on the side table, his granny says, 'Tung over di TV fi-mi nuh.'

Natty-Nya puts down the cup and steps over to the TV. He twists the knob—tissssherrr, tissssherrr, tisssssherrr. 'Hey Granny, tell me when to stop, you know.'

With a few more turns of the silver knob, Natty-Nya is told to stop. An old John Wayne western movie appears on the screen.

'So is dat it Granny?'

She licks her lips and stares at her grandson for a moment or two, then slowly moves over to her drink; even slower still she takes a sip. 'Nuh badda tink seh yuh old granny nuh know weh yuh a keep up outta road.' She puts back down her drink.

Natty-Nya raises his eyebrows and turns up his lips. 'How you mean, Granny?'

'How yuh mean, whey mi mean, ee? Mi seh mi hear weh yuh a gwan wid, a beat up man, rab man and a gwaan wid bare badness, ee? Mine yuh nuh, caah yuh couldda loose yuh life out deh.' Natty-Nya's granny uses her lips again to point at the window.

Natty-Nya squints just like how his dad squints.

The imprint of his jawline shows through his skin. He almost sucks his teeth but he keeps his respectful tone. 'Nah, Granny dat can't happen to me. I'm a bad man on road, Granny.'

Natty-Nya's smug smile meets his granny's cocked eye.

'Bad man, nuh?' says his granny. 'Ju nuh hear weh ol' time people seh?' She points at Natty-Nya with her walking stick. 'Deh always wann badda man out deh fi a man. Memba!'

'Granny just cool, man.' Natty-Nya kisses his granny on the forehead. 'Nuttin' can't happen to me.'

Natty-Nya's granny doesn't reply; she leans back over and picks up her drink as Natty-Nya leaves the room.

Chapter Seven

The sun shines down raw and hot on Brockwell Park. Brixton's biggest park, which was bought from a wealthy family in the 1900s by the government who had ideas of it being a place of tranquility where one, can have peaceful walks within the natural environment for generations to come.

Natty-Nya and his friends menacingly walk through the crowded park—that has an assorted mix of music thundering through it—as they search for the Skin Heads. Natty-Nya and his friends halt in their stride. Natty-Nya sucks his teeth as he spots a group of black men from Clapham Junction.

A week before, Natty-Nya and his friends all went to a party in Clapham Junction. They got into some beef over a real pretty girl and ended up beating down her brother. The brother and his friends from Clapham Junction have now come to get revenge.

Natty-Nya looks calm as he flicks away what is left of his spliff. He taps his best-friend in the chest then leads him and the rest of his friends over to the men from Clapham Junction.

The moment Natty-Nya looks in the eyes of the men from Clapham Junction he knows they don't have what it takes.

Without even blinking an eyelid he knocks out flat the biggest man from Clapham Junction. The rest of the men each take a small step back, and if any of them are wishing they could turn back the hands of time and never have stepped into the park, it is too late. After a spine chilling war cry, out come ratchets and iron poles, which were originally meant for the Skin Heads. The men from Clapham Junction do their best to defend themselves with what weapons they have but the sheer spirit to win by Natty-Nya and his friends is too overwhelming. Bones are crushed. Litres of blood—and even some urine—sink into the grass. The MC on the stage shouts for peace whilst women and children scream and run as Dennis Brown's *"Stop the fussing and fighting"* echoes through the park.

The men from Clapham Junction are saved by "Da Boy-Dem" as they storm into the park with their team of dogs and horses. After a few bites and arrests, the park is left half empty, and as the sun comes down, another beautiful day has been tarnished by mindless violence.

Chapter Eight

Ram Jam on the Brixton Road is jam packed after the violence at the park. Ram Jam is a local blues night-spot which never plays blues music, only reggae. Tonight is no different. The dwellers are raving to music played by the rulers of the sound system, for many years, Brixton-based Sir Coxson International.

The walls of the club are perspiring. Condensation is dripping from the ceiling. The atmosphere is stuffy, hot and stinking of an assortment of perfume and cologne. Coxson takes the crowd to fever pitch with the selection of records they're playing, guaranteeing that ear drums would be ringing for a few days to come from the high wattage they're blasting through the club.

As the music pumps its way through the crowd of sweaty people, it lands on Natty-Nya and his group of friends, all looking trash and ready. They have sexy women grinding on them and a crate full of beer at their feet. Then, like a planned effort, they all say 'BO!' as a fresh Dennis Brown dub plate is played. This brings the house down and forces Coxson to replay the tune. On the third play of the dub, Natty-Nya's best friend turns to him and shouts, 'Rahtid. Yes, mi lion, we make dem boy dem run like puss today. Pussyhole Junction man dem, try big up dem self.'

Natty-Nya nods and sips on his beer, then points the bottle at his best friend. He moves forward to his friend's ear and says, 'Don't make dat fool you, today dey run like puss, tomorrow dey strong like lion. So before dey can get strong like lion we have to make sure dey understand dat Brixton run tings and always will. So if we have to kill dem.' Natty-Nya breaks into patios. 'A suh it guh. Man fi dead, seen.'

Natty-Nya moves back and looks square in the eyes of his best friend to see if he understands the significance of what he had just said. His best friend raises his fist and touches it onto Natty-Nya's fist. 'Yeah, man, Brixton run tings fi years widout tears, no pussy test!'

Natty-Nya slowly nods. 'Ah, so you overstand, but first we have to deal wid dem dutty racists Skin Heads. Den we need to get organized and form a posse, cos we could run da whole of London like dem old white gangsters Jack Spot and Billy Hill use to do back in da day. True-true.'

The moment Natty-Nya utters those last words, Dennis Brown's *"Revolution"* is spun back for the fourth time and the men from Clapham Junction, now simply called Junction Man, become Brixton's mortal enemies for the next two decades.

1980's

Chapter Nine

When '81 had kicked in, the Rastafarian ideology of *"Bunning down Babylon"* had materialized. Black people stopped fighting amongst themselves and made Britain suffer the worst riot in British history. The Brixton riot had started from "Da Boy-Dem's" suss law, which basically meant the police could arrest an individual, mostly young blacks, and send them to prison just on suspicion. The police sent Natty-Nya and many of his friends to prison using the suss law and this resulted in them becoming career criminals. As they saw it, if they're going to be sent to prison for not committing a crime they might as well commit a crime to be sent to prison for.

The aftermath of the riots had left the same scars on buildings that the Second World War had left four decades ealier. Natty-Nya and his friends were some of the frontline soldiers that were throwing petrol bombs, burning out police cars, digging up pavements and using the slabs to crack open police officers' heads.

A young boy with a pretty flat nose rushes to his bedroom window and sees Natty-Nya jumping over his back garden gate as he is chased by "Da Boy-Dem". For a second the young boy is scared but then hopes Natty-Nya will get away, wishing he were old enough to help him escape. The young boy almost says, 'Dutty Babylon fi dead,' but dares not because his mum is standing right behind him.

After the '81 riots, black gangs begin to form in Brixton; the first one being Natty-Nya's gang the Raiders Posse, followed by the Younger Raiders, the Wacka Posse, the Hangman Posse and a few smaller firms. During 1983 and 1984, all the Brixton firms came together to form the Brixton Massive, a force to be reckoned with, that the National Front quickly discovers. The National Front better known as the N.F decides, one sunny afternoon, to march down Brixton Road, a road built by the Romans, with their Nazi flags and police protection. Well, the Brixton Massive isn't having any of it; they throw missiles of bricks and bottles and run those small-minded ignorant souls out of Brixton along with their protection.

"FIRE, FIRE, FIRE," chants the Brixton Massive as the N.F run for their life.

"Believe me, dread, dem N.F must dead, iyah," says Tony Gunn to one of his gang members, Garry Bailey.

"Dem and da Babylon need to dead," responds Garry Bailey.

"Mmm, trust me, iyah," says Tony Gunn.

"But look though, how we gonna rob tonight wid so much beast on da road?"

"Don't watch dat, we're gonna rob tonight," states

Tony Gunn.

The moment night falls on the streets of Brixton, Tony Gunn, Garry Bailey and a few members of the massive, hit the streets, wearing their suede three stripe trainers and some sporting three quarter length coats while others don bomber jackets. They tie their chequered scarfs around their face as they spot their first victim—the pug face broad shouldered white man has no time to respond, his nose cracks under the force of Tony Gunn's foot, the victim slumps to his knees. The blade of a rusty butterfly knife shoots through the victim's skin and crunches onto one of his ribs making the tip of the blade break off into his body. Blows rain down on the defenseless victim. Just before he loses consciousness the last words he hears are: 'Brixton is for blacks, get out and stay out!"

From that night on, Tony Gunn, Garry Bailey and the Brixton Massive commit a string of brutal robberies against white people, their destructive actions fueled out of the anger from the treatment of the police and the hate from the N.F. But like that helpless victim they almost killed, they would usually take it out on the wrong individuals. Nevertheless, their crusade was so ruthless and brutal that after the '85 riots it was their generation that ended racism in the London district of Brixton—which was known back in 1067 as Brixistan, which meant at the stone of Brihtsige. These stones were once used as a meeting point for communities but now, those stones and Brixton's white ancestral communities had long gone leaving Brixton as a no-go-area after dark for white people for the next fifteen years.

Chapter Ten

Da'son had always predicted that there would be many more battles before the war would be won but not even he could have predicted that the battles would have lasted three decades. So much bloodshed just to be able to walk on the street without the fear of attack because one was black.

Da'son thought back to those early days when white people dubbed Somerleyton in Brixton "Little Jamaica". This was even before Brixton's world famous market became invaded with Caribbean food and new black families begun to spring up. Da'son wonders if they could have foreseen that Brixton, on a summer day, would feel like Kingston, Jamaica. Would they have gone a step further past Enoch Powell's speech "Rivers Of Blood" and demanded compulsory repatriation?

However Da'son would go on to tell his grandchildren how those early summer days on the streets of Brixton had a great vibe to it. That whenever a black person (whether they came from the Caribbean or Africa) wanted to get away from seeing racist faces they would come to Brixton and just see black faces (and a few white faces, too) that had a smile for them.

Da'son would carry on telling his grandchildren that on seeing the unity spirit of black people in Brixton and the surrounding areas "Da Boy-Dem" skillfully used the divide and conquer tactic. They packed off groups of black families to populate other areas in London and England, such as: Peckham, Lewisham, Streatham, Wandsworth, Croydon, Thornton Heath, New Cross, Battersea, Harlesden, Tottenham, Ladbroke Grove, Hackney, Bristol, Birmingham and Manchester.

So by the time his grandchildren grew up, black people (sometimes) only had smiles for those from their area, and anyone who didn't come from their area, their bits, their ends, their town, their city, was regarded as an enemy.

For years, before understanding the divide and conquer tactic, Da'son had blamed himself for the younger generation taking his bad man mentality (which should only be used to stand up for justice from the system or racism) out of context and using it against themselves.

He had thought after all the blood that was shed between him and the Teddy Boys to make the streets of Brixton—London safe for the new generation, no more blood would shed. Certainly not black blood by black hands. He had honestly thought that they would know their self-worth and become great conscious beings.

Instead, what Da'son calls "The Brixton Mentality" took over. He would say this came from the divide and conquer tactic, and a twisted version of his bad man mentality, which he felt was a remnant of the psychology from the spirit of the runaway slaves who had to become violent to escape their cruel white captors.

Da'son's blood had always boiled when hearing some white people claim that "The Brixton Mentality" is nothing more than genetics, which was inherited from the black slave ancestry characteristics. This means even if a black man was born and brought up by white people in a remote countryside in Russia and was never exposed to black culture or even seen another black person he would still act ignorant and kill a man if a man stepped on his shoe, or screwed him for too long.

Da'son would always tell his grandchildren not to believe this because before their ancestors were beaten, sold and shipped half way around the world they were dancing to their African drums, eating plenty of good food and living in love.

Chapter Eleven

The year is now 1988. The Lion Men have disappeared from "The Frontline", replaced by Natty-Nya's generation, called Line Man, because they hang out on "The Frontline". They have turned that strip of road into a no go area night or day for anyone, even the police. "The Frontline" resembles the wild-wild-west; anything goes: drugs, murder, prostitution, extortion and robbery.

A woman screams. Her handbag is ripped off her shoulder at the corner of Coldharbour Lane and "Frontline". A rookie policeman blows his whistle and is now in hot pursuit of the young street robber.

The young street robber is slim and tall. His legs are long and he has the fitness of a top athlete. With every stride he takes, whizzing past the various smells on "The Frontline" from Jamaican Patti and Harddough bread to Ganja, he is leaving the Rookie further and further behind. The Rookie realises that he won't be able to catch the robber and decides to radio in for back up. When he is asked his location, he stammers back R-Railton Road. He is promptly told to cease his pursuit.

He stops in his tracks, his eyebrows scrunch together and his mouth drops open. The street robber stops and gives the officer the finger and shouts, 'You pussyhole, go suck your mudda.'

The street robber turns around laughing. Then with the bottom of his trousers tucked into his diamond patterned socks, he freely bops with his stolen loot into one of Railton Road's sanctuaries: Dexter Road Adventure Playground, which is simply called Dexter.

The young street robber, who everyone calls Slu, steps in among his large group of friends, gassing, but really hoping that the purse will contain a fair amount of money. 'Oi you lot,' says Slu, 'I just licked a tek, init, raggo. And one radie try run me down, init.'

An older head, called Wizzy, from the Younger Raiders and the Brixton Massive, steps in among the young men who are surrounding Slu and listening to his story of escape. Wizzy says to Slu, 'What da Babylon dem try run you down?' This isn't a question. 'Which part of da line did da radie stop running you down?'

Slu flicks his hand towards outside. 'Just outside, init.'

'Seen… You know why da radie stop running you down, init?'

Slu looks blankly at Wizzy, who says, 'Because of me and my generation, init. We mek di Babylon dem scared fi come up here by demselves. So da way I see it dat tek should be mines, star.'

Wizzy reaches out to take the loot. Slu pulls it away. 'Wot da rass you doing? Oi, Wizzy mine wot you're doing you nah, star? Wot you think um some little yute dat you can bad up? Listen, you're a chief, man.'

Wizzy raises his finger as if to poke Slu in the side of his head. 'How you mean mine wot I'm doing, watch how you're talking to me you know, Slu, because you're a little yute.' Wizzy points his finger towards Slu's eye. 'Listen, don't think dat you're bad, you know, cos you're sparring wid your Younger Hangman Posse.'

Slu and his crew look at Wizzy in astonishment. Slu laughs. 'Dat's why I know you're a fool, you chief. We ain't called no Younger Hangman, you sell out.'

Wizzy kisses his teeth. 'Seen. So wot are you fools called den?'

Slu doesn't respond straightaway, then says, 'Just cool, man you idiot. Don't worry wot we're called.'

Wizzy laughs and whips his hand towards Slu's face missing it by inches. 'Cos you lot aren't called nufin'.'

Wizzy is about to walk off when Natty-Nya, who had been waiting to sell some weed and listening from the edge of the playground, steps up. 'Oi, Wizzy leave da yute dem alone, wot der rass is wrong wid you, ee?'

Fear reaches Wizzy's eyes; he bows his head and says nothing. Natty-Nya runs his hand through his neatly kept dreadlocks, then swoops his gaze over Slu and his mates. Natty-Nya and Slu are cousins. Slu's great granny is first cousin to Natty-Nya's granny. Both men are unaware of this fact. Natty-Nya counts Slu and his friends. He stops at twenty-eight, looks over at Wizzy, and says, 'Dey're called da 28s, dat's wot dey're called, da 28s, so 'member.'

And just like that, the Brixton 28s are born.

Late Summer 1992

Chapter Twelve

'28s say we're great, say we're great, say we're great. 28s, say we're...' Slu points two fingers rhythmically at one of his gang members and continues the second line to his rap. '28s, posse, posse, posse, posse...' Slu is abruptly stopped from continuing his rap by a short dark-skin stocky yute from Clapham Junction who steps out of the toilet cubicle and steps on Slu's foot.

'Oi!' shouts Slu.

The stocky yute turns around and screws up his face, then sucks his teeth.

For a moment Slu is taken aback. He makes eye contact with the yute and tries to read him. Slu doesn't see in the yute what it takes to defeat him. He points his index finger at the yute then at his feet. 'Hold on, star, you just stepped on my foot, you know.'

The yute shouts, 'So wot!'

Stunned, but not really shocked, Slu laughs and looks over at his three other gang members, who he robbed a shop till with earlier. They're celebrating while they wait for the weed man to roll up in the dance.

One of the gang members says, 'Hold on, he's going on like he's dark!'

In the split second that the word dark left the gang member's lips, Slu takes out what can only best be described as homemade pepper spray, which they called jiff back in the day.

Slu "jiffs" the stocky yute; the yute cries and runs for the door. He makes it out before they can grab him back in and stamp on his head.

Holding his face, the yute runs into the crowd of ravers; the crowd opens up then closes. Slu and the other gang members all buckle into the dance hall. They're unable to see where the yute has run to, so they decide to flush him out and at the same time "done da dance".

They spray the dance with CS gas; a scream is heard, then a few more. The gas takes hold, choking the nearest people to where it was first sprayed. A few minutes later it has spread to the whole dance; everyone is choking, and with eyes burning they stampede to the inadequate exit, with the sound of Tenor Saw's *"Ring the alarm"* blazing through the speakers.

Chapter Thirteen

The young boy with the pretty flat nose is one of the last ravers to step out of the Bogle Factory, an empty warehouse on Somerleyton Road named after the Bogle dance that was created by the late dancing genius, Mr Bogle.

The boy calmly walks further into the fresh air. The bottom end of his jeans are rolled up and tied tightly to his ankles making them rest neatly on top of his basketball boots. CS gas no longer throws him into a state of panic; he is use to it from being in countless raves that were gassed in the past. Outside people are still choking and hoping they can return back into the rave. They all want to continue enjoying the music that *Nasty Love*, the best Brixton sound system in the 90s, was playing with special guest *Tim Westwood* (the only white man that the pretty flat nose boy ever saw come down by himself at night to one of Brixton's roughest night clubs, *Steppers*).

Slu and his friends are standing with five other 28s; one of the five apparently knows the stocky yute and convinces Slu that he's safe, so Slu decides to hold it down and squash the beef.

If nothing else kicks off outside, it seems as if the rave will continue and the boy with the pretty flat nose can go back to crubbing down the det girl he had on the wall.

Unfortunately, this will not be happening because the stocky yute has come to this rave to settle a grudge with Slu. Two weeks earlier another Brixton gang called the Untouchables—who were always at war with the 28s—had robbed and beaten up the stocky yute's little brother. When word got back to the stocky yute he only heard that it was some boys from Brixton, and maybe Peckham, then somewhere down the line Slu's name was mentioned, maybe due to his ghetto fame.

The stocky yute appears from around the corner.

'Hey, pussyhole!'

Slu and the rest of the 28s all turn around.

'Wot you say me and you go one on one and lets see if you can handle me like you handle your butters girl.'

One of the 28s cries out, 'Rah, stop dat! He's taking liberties, don't make him take liberties.'

Calmly, Slu smiles, rises off his yellow and black moped, and steps towards the stocky yute. He uses his hand as an imaginary gun and points. 'Oi, mind how you're talking, you know, cos you will lose your shirt and get hurt. Mind I dun your dance out ere.'

'Wot! You think I'm scared of you?' The stocky yute pulls out a knife.

Slu raises his eyebrows, and the look of the grim reaper enters his eyes.

There is one thing that most people from different ends have to learn about the 28s. To the 28s there is nothing like a fair fight. If you are fighting one, you are fighting all of them and all of them have grown from twenty-eight to hundreds. The 28s have spread into the other two surrounding towns so there is now the Clapham 28s and the Stockwell 28s. This means the moment the stocky yute pulls out his knife, he pulls it out on every 28s gang member.

Blood pours. From every angle the yute tries to escape to he runs into a tip of a blade. The yute gets the chance to make a run for it but is chased and stabbed at the same time. He is stabbed into a shop and stabbed out of it. The stabs do not cease until the yute runs back up the road where he first took out his knife, and finally collapses.

Chapter Fourteen

The boy with the pretty flat nose looks down on the dying yute and the paramedics trying to save his life. The boy can't help thinking, *did this yute come here tonight to end his life?*

His thoughts cease as his attention is drawn to a white female paramedic who has the dying yute's right arm held up in the air. She frantically shouts: 'We're losing him!'

The boy peers over her shoulder and looks into the eyes of the dying yute. The boy suddenly realises by the sheer determination in the stocky yute's eyes that he desperately wants to live. The stocky yute had been sent to England from Nigeria because of his bad behavior, and his parents felt that "non-violent" good old England would make him into a better person. Maybe this is what his ancestors had felt when they sold one of his unruly ancestors to the English who brought the ancestor to Jamaica to chop sugar cane. But what is really strange is that this ancestor, who had to slave from sunup to sundown, was a direct ancestor to Slu.

The boy with the pretty flat nose averts his gaze

from the stocky yute, then looks at his trail of blood; thick and still hot. Soon it will be cold then faded into the concrete like so many people who've had their blood spilled on the streets of Brixton. The boy leaves the murder scene as an air ambulance comes to pick up the stocky yute. The night rings out with police sirens. There is no more 28s on the road, and no one would ever be charged for this murder, guaranteeing the 28s name would be feared for many more years to come.

The fear for the 28s ended with the invasion of the Jamaican gangsters who called themselves Shottas, but who all the yutes called "Yardies." The yutes ended up calling everyone who sold drugs Shotters because they heard the "Yardies" call themselves Shottas, and then saw them selling crack and calling it a "shot".

The "Yardies", although not their first attempt, had practically taken over the underworld of Brixton and it seemed as if the 28s had disappeared. Well, most had, due to being locked up in prison or dead. The "Yardies" had seized the opportunity and with their guns as their main muscle, they were able to steal the man-dem's women and turn the weak into crack heads.

Brixton has become "Little Jamaica" once more. Almost every yute is dressing like the "Yardies", talking like them and wants to be them. And one man, Rockne, set it all off.

Rockne is a notorious bad man from the ghettos of Jamaica who has been expelled from America but has plans to spread destruction and more death on the streets of Brixton.

Winter
Jamaica 1992

Chapter Fifteen

Rockne stands in his one bedroom shack with the scent of burning rubbish flowing through the small open window.

Since being deported from America he has lost everything. But that doesn't matter now because he has a Visa to enter England, and a great crack cocaine connection—the Captain of an airplane who flies into Britain with kilograms of the poison and drops it off at a posh hotel in the West End of London. So Rockne plans on getting everything back that he had in America, plus more, or die trying.

His woman places his last pair of jeans in the suitcase. As she zips it up she says, 'Suh, yuh a guh sen fi mi when yuh reach?'

Rockne doesn't answer. He thinks he hears something and looks over at the door. He does hear something; it is a young boy named Thomas, who idolizes Rockne and who later in life will name himself "Tommy Terrible".

Thomas keeps as still as possible until Rockne stops looking at the door.

Rockne answers his woman as he sits down on the bed. 'Cool nuh, mammy, man. Mi nuh tell yuh seh mi a guh sen fi yuh when mi reach, jus cool nuh, man.'

Rockne's woman walks over to her man and rubs his head. 'A'rite babes, mi ah mek sure.'

Rockne gives his woman a kiss. 'Cool nuh mammy, man, mi nuh tell yuh, man.'

Rockne's woman goes back to rubbing his head. 'An' be careful babes, caah mi nuh waan't nuhbady fi tell mi seh nuttun duh yuh.'

Rockne sucks his teeth and pulls his woman in front of him. 'Weh mi say, Hingland saaf, nuttun cyaan duh mi, mi a bad man.' Rockne stands up from his bed. 'Yuh nuh memba bout di story, back inna di fiftys when yardman mash up Hingland, mi hear seh a one-man responsible fi dat. And mi know seh him could a neva bad lackka mi.' Rockne picks up his shirt and slips it on over his arms. 'Nuh worry, nuttun cyaan duh mi, mi agguh tek ova Hingland, man. Mek bare money, den when mi dunn mi agguh come back a yawd an mek yuh live life.'

Thomas accidentally knocks off the bin lid. Dogs start barking. Rockne steps to the door and shouts, 'Hey bowy cum outta mi yawd, mi tell yuh seh fi nuh cum inyah?'

Thomas doesn't look back. His heart pounds and his mind dwells over the England bad man story. One day, he thinks, he will make it to England and join Rockne as another bad yardman.

A Year Later

Chapter Sixteen

Rockne had made it into England, and as planned took over Brixton. He had to pay a few hardcore black English gangsters to leave him in peace while he turned the weak-minded into cats and brought Brixton to its knees.

One dark night he enters a house party on Coldharbour Lane to rob some shotters. The house has tall steps leading to a blue door; the windows are vibrating from the bassy music. Rockne barges in by himself with two rusty guns. He smashes the biggest man with the biggest chain on his nose, using the butt of the gun. The man falls into the room. The dancing stops. The DJ pulls up the music, and Rockne turns on the light. There are about twenty-five people in the large room that permeates with the smell of brandy and weed. Out of the twenty-five there are four shotters. Rockne lines them up. 'Unnu line up!'

The shotters look at each other with eyes wide and expressions blank. Rockne kicks the man he knocked on the floor. 'Hey, sucka bolo, mi seh line up.'

The man drags himself off the floor and stands in

line with the other shotters as blood runs down his face, then onto his silk suit and suede shoes. 'Yow dan a how yuh ah gawn suh?'

Rockne puts one of his guns in the waist of his over-sized-pocket corduroy suit. Then says, 'How yuh mean, a mi run di drug business inna Brixtan. MI!' Rockne pokes his gun in his chest. 'Mi bumboclaat run dis. Yeah, an mi nuh love how unnu a mek money an nah pay nuh tax.'

The shotters would be scratching their heads, if they could, because they didn't know they had to pay Rockne. With a sinister smirk on his face that makes his eyebrows crease together, Rockne walks over to the biggest man. 'Hey my yute, tek haf yuh chain.'

The man doesn't think twice; he pulls off his chain. Rockne sticks it in his over-sized pocket. He walks to the next man, then the next, telling them to take off their chain or chops. No one argues.

'Unnu memba da warning yah, unnu know weh mi deh, mi waah suttum once a week.' Rockne runs his eyes over the line of shotters. He huffs. 'Mi dunn talk, memba, mi a gun dawg!'

Rockne lets off a shot. BAM! The bullet flies through the ceiling, then up through a bed in which a young boy was sleeping in just five minutes ago until he decided to venture downstairs. The young boy doesn't flinch as the gunshot goes off. He just hops back on the stairs with thoughts of being old enough to get a gun to shoot down this Jamaican man. From this moment on the young boy forms a hatred for all "Yardies."

1996

Chapter Seventeen

The "Yardie" invasion has ended. Rockne left his gun at home and was consequently gunned down while collecting his tax from a shotter. The rest of Rockne's crew try to keep control. But the moment converted, replica and deactivated guns—Rebores—hit the street, taking the price of a weapon of destruction from thousands down to under a hundred, black British yutes reclaim back the streets. Only this time there is something different about these black yutes in Brixton. These yutes see the world of a gangster in a different light. This comes apparent as three yutes run into Slu's sister's home, a new council flat built at the back of "Frontline", escaping from a bank robbery. The yutes run into the brown-painted kitchen that stinks of bacon, shouting with excitement. Money drops out of their clothes but before they can pick it up, in walks an original 28 named Paro; Slu's sister's boyfriend. Paro is Natty-Nya's nephew and also unaware that him and Slu are cousins, which means that he doesn't know he's going out with his own cousin.

'Oi, rudeboy, wot da hell are you lot doing, running

up in my yard like dis, rudeboy?' demands Paro.

The yutes pick up their stolen money. One of them says, 'We just licked da Abbey init, shabby.'

Paro steps forward. 'Rudeboy, I can see dat, rude-boy, but why run up in my yard, rudeboy?'

The same yute who spoke before says, 'We didn't even know dis was your yard, thingy open da door for us, init.'

'Who's thingy, rudeboy? Who, my girl?'

'Yeah, isn't dis her yard?'

Paro sucks his teeth. 'Forget bout dat, rudeboy, when I'm here dis is my yard, rudeboy, and anything in it, is mines. D'you get me, rudeboy?'

The yutes tighten their grip on the money. Paro smiles. 'But just cool yeah, rudeboy, just give me half of wot you lot got dere and it's all good. D'you get me, rudeboy?'

The yutes think if they should challenge Paro or not, but it seems as if they all, at the exact same time, remember that Paro has a reputation as a mad man. They are about to split their lick when the young boy who had the bullet fly through his bed, steps into the kitchen.

'Oi, you lot don't make him try set you,' says the young boy, who is first cousins with Slu, which means he is also Paro's cousin and doesn't know.

Paro turns around, sucks his teeth. 'Wot! Oi, Gunn don't try roll up in here like you're ruff, you know, rudeboy.'

'Shut up, you dick head, you're too red-eye, man.' The young boy pushes out his chest. 'Wot, you can't tell me nufin', you're a plum, man. You're a fool,' says the young boy who everybody calls Gunn due him taking over the reins of badness when his older half-brother Tony Gunn took Slu on a house burglary that went wrong and they both got life sentences.

Paro angrily says, 'Oi, rudeboy, you should laow da tuff talk, you know, rudeboy. Cos you're forgetting yourself and who brought you. D'you get me, rudeboy? Member how you got your name on road, rudeboy. If it weren't for me, your big brother and Slu paving da way, you lot wouldn't be da younger, younger, younger 28s. D'you get me, rudeboy?'

Gunn sucks his teeth. 'Forget bout dat, all of you lot drop offa shape from long time, you lot all made da Yardies come over here and take over.' Gunn sucks his teeth again. 'You lot days are done. You're wash.' Gunn pauses. His eyes become slits as he pulls out a .38 caliber pistol, and with pure conviction, says, 'Listen, dis is a new era, dere is no more 28s, no more snakes; it's now da Peel-Dem Crew with 38s.'

Chapter Eighteen

Gunn, like most of the yutes that followed in the wake of Natty-Nya, has become a devoted gang member and has grown up with "The Brixton Mentality", which now is represented in one sentence: *I'm from Brixton, so I'm a bad man.*

"The Brixton Mentality" was thrust upon most of them from an early age by their older siblings or relatives. Before Gunn reached the age of eleven he had robbed someone with a ratchet knife. By the time he reached twelve he knew how to use nunchakus, and just wished he could have stolen his uncle's gun, which he had seen lying beside him as he counted out his drug money; Gunn had thought that on his first day of secondary school. He would carry the gun in his waist and when the time came for him to declare that he was from Brixton so therefore he's a bad man, he would coolly reveal the gun for proof.

Gunn was even excited that one day he would end up in prison. That one day he would end up just like some of the elders with no education or job. Gunn's dream whilst growing up went no further than robbing, getting a mobile and selling drugs, killing—if need be—and smoking weed all day. But things might have been different for Gunn when one day he and his half-brother, Tony Gunn bump into the boy with the pretty flat nose.

Tony Gunn says to the boy, 'Wot, are you going college? Rah you sold it, you're a sell out.'

These words pierce the boy's soul, making him question himself: *am I really selling out? Should I be going on like I'm too bad for the world, too bad for anyone whether they're from the US, Jamaica or anywhere else?*

The boy smiles at Tony Gunn as he remembers something he read in a book, which said: *an individual is not great simply because he is black or white. An individual is great depending on his will to use his creative ability to create great values that will enrich and benefit others.*

The boy then casually, but with a powerful tone, says, 'I'm not selling out, but soon I will be selling a great value that I will have created after I have left college. Over-stand that.'

Tony Gunn doesn't reply as he absorbs the significance of the sentence. But because he feels he has gone too far with his destructive lifestyle and cannot turn back he shrugs off a decision that could have changed his destiny and the destiny of his little half-brother.

He walks off with Gunn telling him, 'College and education are for pussies; crime and guns are for bad boys, and you're gonna be a bad boy, right?'

'Yeah, yeah,' says Gunn as he skips up behind his half-brother.

PART TWO

PART TWO

The 21st Century
Jamaica: Tenement Yard

Chapter Nineteen

The sun has not yet come up and begun to beat down its electrifying heat on the little island of Jamaica when Thomas, the little boy who had been listening to Rockne all those years ago, opens his eyes. Thomas is the son of a woman who is the love child of Da'son. This makes him Natty-Nya's nephew, Paro's first cousin, and unbeknownst to him, a distant cousin to Gunn.

Thomas has now grown into a young man. He has just finished college where he earned a diploma in electronics, but he cannot let go of his dream to travel to England and become a notorious bad man. He has heard of Rockne's success and demise but that still doesn't faze him.

Thomas jumps out of the bunk bed and stretches. He looks down at his sister. She opens her eyes and says, 'Wey yuh a guh suh early, ee?'

Thomas slaps his chest. 'Cool nuh, man, mi nuh tell yuh lass nite mi hav fi get up early fi check mi breddrin dung a Jungle?'

Thomas's sister's eyes widens with shock. 'Wait,

yuh tell mammy seh yuh nah guh dung deh fi mix up wid di bad breed dem.'

Thomas puts his finger to his lips. 'Shhhh, yuh waan mammy fi hear weh yuh a seh?'

'No,' replies Thomas's sister in a low remorseful voice.

'TAMAS!' hollers his mum.

Thomas pinches his sister's arm. 'Shit, yuh si it?' Thomas looks towards his door and bites his lip. He is about to answer when the door is pushed open letting in the scent of freshly cooked ackee and salt fish. 'Tamas, yuh nuh hear mi a call yuh?' demands his mum.

Thomas walks towards his shirt. 'Yes, mammy, I wuz cuming.'

Thomas's mum places her hand on her large hip. 'Member seh yuh flight a leff two a clack, suh a whey yuh a guh?'

Thomas puts on his shirt. 'Mammy, mi haffi guh dung a Half Wey Tree.'

'Wey mek yuh haffi guh a Half Wey Tree faah?'

Quickly and smooth, Thomas rolls the lie off his tongue. 'Mammy mi tell yuh mi haffi pick up sumtings fi a jab when mi reach a Hingland.' Thomas rolls his eyes to his sister to see if she's going to give him away with a bait expression. His sister has her eyes closed.

'A'rite, mek sure when yuh reach Hingland yuh behave yuh self, wuk hard, caz mi neva wuk an sell tripe a markit an clean people house fi nuttun. Suh mi nuh waah hear seh yuh tun bad man a Hingland.'

Thomas looks towards the ground. 'Nah mammy,

man, mi naah duh dat, mi agguh behave mi self an mek nuff money, den cum back an mek yuh live life.'

Thomas's mum smiles. 'Cum yah, mi one son.' She holds the back of her son's head and says a prayer.

Thomas looks over at his sister and warns her with a look not to say anything about his real plans; she understands and says a little prayer for herself.

A Day Later
Brixton: London

Chapter Twenty

The face of Brixton resembles a trendy middle-class London district far removed from the aftermath of the first riot. Back then, and into the early nineties, no investors or businesses wanted to come to Brixton. But when the street robberies stopped and the drug selling began, investors and businesses flooded the area.

Some people would say Brixton has never been a bad place; well, it isn't a bad place as long as one is a legal, hardworking member of society. But the moment one decides to make money illegally from the streets, Brixton suddenly becomes a living hell.

The boy with the pretty flat nose has now become a man. He stops to wait for his bus, which is opposite a mosque. The doors of the mosque open and out steps Gunn dressed in black. He is followed by ten others who used to be in his Peel Dem Crew (PDC). Gunn had ended his PDC days shortly after he became Muslim. He gave the reigns over to the younger yutes who still gang bang while others make music, calling themselves Poverty Driven Children (PDC).

Nowadays, Gunn and his Muslim brothers who trail behind him are called "The Muslim Boys" by the media and police. They are blamed for terrorizing the streets of Brixton, and they are accused of using their newly-adopted faith out of context, to rationalize robbing and killing non-Muslims.

Looking from across the road, the man with the pretty flat nose shakes his head and thinks: *what if this group of yutes grow into an army, what would this mean for London, England? What if one of these yutes become a competent leader and begin to spread the physical violent term of Jihad out of Brixton? Would England's government and its dominant faith be in serious trouble?*

The man carefully looks at Gunn to see if he could be the one to make this happen. A chill comes over him as he senses Gunn may have the potential.

Gunn smiles, then puts his phone in his pocket. He picks out four of his Muslim brothers who follow him to his car.

The man with the pretty flat nose watches as they walk away, into the night, with an aura that exudes no fear of man or death.

Chapter Twenty-One

Gunn and his Muslim brothers drive down Brixton Road, then up Acre Lane. They are now waiting at their destination inside a car mixed with a perfumed, aromatic and fried chicken smell.

Ten minutes have passed, and what they're waiting for has not yet turned up. Gunn looks at one of his Muslim brothers. 'Oi, akhi, pass me da mash.'

His Muslim brother gives Gunn a heavy silver pistol. Gunn rolls it around in his palm. 'Listen,' he says, addressing all of the Muslim brothers. 'Naam, if we have to lick dis doughnut down, den we have to lick him down, inshallah. You listening? We need to forget dat he's old school. At da end of da day, he had his chance to become a brudder.'

In agreement to Gunn's statement, the rest of his Muslim brothers say, 'True stories, akhi!'

Gunn picks up on the agreement. 'Inshallah. So just remember, he's a kuffar and his money needs to be taken and brought into the ways of Allah.' Gunn's Muslim brothers nod, and in that very moment, the front door, which they had been watching, opens.

Out steps Peon. He's one of those criminals who has never been to prison and always wins his court cases. So in the eyes of society, he could still be looked upon as a decent law-abiding citizen, and could even get a job serving the Queen tea. Peon has a bag hung over his shoulder, which he grips tightly. He walks with his eyes darting around, looking for his ride.

Gunn places his hand on the car door handle, and says to his Muslim brothers, 'Remember, no love for da faithless. Allahu Akbar.'

Gunn and his Muslim brothers jump out the car. Gunn points his gun at Peon. 'Oi, my yute, don't move!'

Peon's eyes widen. He freezes and loses the ability to speak.

With a determining look in his eyes, Gunn says, 'We're here to eat you, inshallah. So, hear wot, either you give man da pees, or man's gonna bun you… One or da two, inshallah.'

Peon has not just lost his voice, but he is lost for words. He can't understand that these guys he'd grown up with, and even robbed with, are now robbing him. With no emotion, Peon removes the bag from his shoulder and gives over £20,000, which he had been saving under his bed.

Gunn takes the bag and says, 'Naam, is dat da pees, yeah? Mashallah.' He opens it, smiles, then sticks his gun into Peon's waist. 'Allahu Akbar.'

Urine runs down Peon's leg, as he holds back his tears of terror and watches Gunn and the rest walk to their car exuding no fear of man or death.

Later That Night

Chapter Twenty-Two

The bedroom is a bit bigger than a prison cell. It smells of a sweet cherry scent. Islamic rugs decorate the walls. There are only two books in the room—both, Holy Korans.

Gunn sits down on his silver sofa bed, and hands the final cut of the money to the last of his Muslim brother who is about to leave his house.

'So wot, you're gonna be here for da rest of da night, ak?' asks his Muslim brother.

Gunn readjusts his jeans and nods. 'Inshallah, akhi, Inshallah.'

'A'ight den, little more from now.' Gunn's Muslim brother spuds him.

'Ma'al salam,' says Gunn.

His Muslim brother turns to leave, opens the door, and replies, 'Baraka Allah.'

Outside, he is met by Gunn's mum; she's a boutique of a woman in stature and still has her beautiful young features. Despite being a mother of four, she could easily be mistaken for Gunn's big sister.

Gunn's Muslim brother bows his head in respect.

'Hello, Miss Gunn.'

Miss Gunn doesn't reply. She almost kisses her teeth, and then cuts her eyes.

Gunn's Muslim brother quickly heads for the front door, and exits the house.

Miss Gunn pushes open Gunn's bedroom door. She folds her arms. 'What have I told you?'

Gunn shrugs. 'Wot, mum, told me wot?'

Miss Gunn bites her bottom lip, her eyes narrowing. She controls her voice. 'I'm sure I told you I don't want to hear no Islam ting in my house.'

'Wot do you mean, mum? Dat's my faith, you know.'

'That's not your faith,' Miss Gunn almost shouts. 'I didn't bring you up no bloody Muslim. You were christened in the Church of God. You're a Christian.'

With conviction, and eyes locked onto his mum's screwed-up face, Gunn replies, 'Not no more, mum, I was lost wid da cross. Islam is da true faith. Der is no God but Allah, Allahu Akbar.' Gunn gets up, picks up his Koran and quickly recites, 'Bismillahir rahmanir rahim.' Then begins reading a passage.

His mum's eyes almost pop out of their sockets. 'Listen—' she points her delicate finger '—don't bother read me nothing from that, yeah.'

Gunn closes the Koran. 'Mum, you're lost. You need to find Islam and become Muslim, inshallah.'

Gunn's mum kisses her teeth. She just can't believe her son, who she went through forty-eight hours of labour for and raised without a father, is telling her how to live her life. Gunn's mum really feels like throwing Gunn out of her house but remembers an old Jamacian saying: *Finger stink? Yuh cyaan dash it wey. Meaning, your kids are your kids no matter what they do, you can't abandon them.*

Gunn's mum sighs. 'I'm not going to talk again,' she says. 'Just take down them things from the wall.'

Miss Gunn closes the bedroom door, leaving Gunn holding his Koran.

Two Days Later

Chapter Twenty-Three

Thomas has just arrived in England and is already finding out what the streets of Brixton might have in store for him. He is sitting with three others in a double bedroom that is decorated with lines of trainers placed at the bottom of the wall. Thomas is listening to Peon retell the robbing.

Peon walks from the window, pointing his crooked fingers towards the floor. 'I swear on da Holy Bible, you know, king, if something isn't done bout dis Muslim ting, we're all gonna be dead, or Muslims. Real talks.' Peon licks his lips. 'I swear down, dem bludclart yutes ain't playin' yah-nah.' Peon squints. 'How can dey roll up on me in broad day light, bruv? All rassclart quotin' da Koran as dey stick their gun in my chest.' Peon kisses his teeth and walks back to the window. He places his palm on the windowsill and stares out.

A voice from behind, says, 'Oi, rudeboy, just cool, man. I told you we're gonna get back your pees for you, just cool, rudeboy.'

Peon turns around to address the voice, which comes from Paro. The same Paro who is unaware that he is Gunn's distant cousin and who still says "Rudeboy" and "d'you get me rudeboy?" throughout his sentences.

Paro gets up. 'Oi, rudeboy, Gunn and dem pussyhole idiot Muslim brothers can't get away wid dis, d'you get me, rudeboy?' Paro raises his eyebrows. 'Yeah, rudeboy. Gunn and dem have been goin' on cold still. But you know wot? Every dog will have his day, d'you get me, rudeboy?' Paro nods. 'And trust me, rudeboy, his day, and da whole of his Muslim gang, soon done. Deir free paper soon bun, d'you get me, rudeboy? Deir bets soon bust. So don't worry, yeah, cuz.'

A call comes through to Paro. He answers his phone. 'Wot…?' You can't get da stick and sweets until tomorrow, rudeboy? Yeah, yeah, a'ight, rudeboy. Peace.' Paro smiles and says to Peon, 'Everything is set for tomorrow, rudeboy, so I'll holla, yeah?'

Peon slowly nods in agreement, but deep down he wants to call off the attack. He just wants to forget about his loss —maybe go to college and become a nine to fiver.

Paro turns to Thomas. 'Come, rudeboy, let me talk to you outside, rudeboy.'

Thomas gets up from the long leather sofa and follows Paro, leaving Peon and two others behind in the blue, laminated floor, bedroom.

Chapter Twenty-Four

Outside is cool and crisp. For a winter month it feels more like a cold summer night.

Paro and Thomas are standing beside Peon's car. Paro lights a spliff. His eyes are red and his clothes already smell of a strong scent of weed. He has been smoking high grade all week as he celebrated his release from prison. Paro was on remand for accessory of drug importation. He had bust the case because the person who got caught with the high grade testified that Paro was not involved. In his lifetime Paro has spent four and a half years behind bars and he still hasn't got a criminal record.

He looks at Thomas who is his first cousin. 'A rudeboy, let me tell you bout certain man in Brixton, rudeboy, secretly—most are dick heads, d'you get me, rudeboy? But dey have dis Brixton ting bout dem, rudeboy, and I'm not talking bout people who just live in Brixton I'm talking bout da man-dem on road, roadman, d'you get me, rudeboy? Secretly—dey think dey should be too bad for da world, rudeboy, 'cos deir from Brixton. So yeah dey will go on bad, but trust me, rudeboy, once you catch dem by demselves, secretly, deir shook ones. D'you get me, rudeboy?' Paro pulls hard on his spliff then causally blows out the smoke. 'Yeah, certain of da man-dem are nufin' wid-out deir team, dey wouldn't even buss deir gun by demselves. D'you get me, rudeboy?'

Paro points his spliff to Thomas. 'So, rudeboy, dat's where you can take advantage…' Paro pauses, licks his lips then squints his eyes. 'Rudeboy, if you want to take over the street…' Paro stops in his sentence as he looks around to the other two men that were left with Peon.

The taller one says, 'Oi, wot's going on old school, you going down to Satay Bar?'

'Yeah, rudeboy,' Paro answers, 'little more from now, init, rudeboy.'

'A'ight, king, I'm gonna go up to da Lane and come back, gee.'

The two men walk off. Paro says to Thomas. 'Come family, let's talk in my car, rudeboy.'

Chapter Twenty-Five

The insides of Paro's black car is kitted out with cream leather. Being in his early thirties and not having any children, his car is his baby. He had started out with a banger when he first began shoting stones back in the mid-nineties, after being on remand for two years.

Paro turns the music to low as the engine fires up and the heated seats begin to warm. He drops his window down a bit and relights his spliff. Paro turns his head to Thomas. 'Rudeboy, you listening?'

Thomas says, 'Yeah, man. Mi ah hear yuh, dawg.'

Paro grips the steering wheel. 'Don't get it twisted, you know, rudeboy. Road can be sticky, especially since dis Muslim ting 'as taken over, d'you get me, rudeboy? Dey're all licking man down if you refuse to become a Muslim, rudeboy.'

Thomas nods. 'Yeah... ah suh dem ah gwan, my lawd?'

'Yeah, rudeboy, grimy but you know wot, rudeboy? I feel say dat if someone takes out dat idiot Gunn da rest will fold cos dey all look up to him and follow him.

D'you get me, rudeboy?'

Thomas looks at Paro. 'Ah suh nuh?'

'Course, rudeboy, all a man has to do is lick down Gunn and da streets is yours. D'you get me, rudeboy?' Paro takes a deep pull on his spliff. 'Listen, rudeboy, let me tell you about Gunn. I've known dat yute since he was young. I use to move wid his big brother, d'you get me, rudeboy? One ting bout him he was never scared to rock anyone no matter how big dey were, d'you get me, rudeboy? Dis could have been because he had no fear or he knew most man would be scared to do him sutum due to his big brother... wotever it was he rose to the top, rudeboy.' Paro darts his eyes out of the window as if he had heard someone approaching his car. He winds the window shut. 'Yeah, so anyway, rudeboy, dat's wot the streets respect, no fear. But, rudeboy, wot I feel right now is you can take over like da Yardies did back in da nineties, d'you get me, rudeboy? Dat's wot Brixton needs another Yardie take over.' Paro laughs.

Thomas smiles. Before this talk with Paro he was beginning to consider that maybe taking over the streets of Brixton would be much harder than he thought. Now he thinks all he has to do is lick down Gunn.

Chapter Twenty-Six

Gunn gets off his knees. He has just finished praying while facing the east. He folds up his praying mat, and is about to pick up his Koran when his bedroom door flies open. Standing in the doorway and whiffing in her freshly-washed iron linen smell is his girlfriend, Cadija. A beautiful, smooth, dark skin sister with eyes that a man can get lost in.

With a pissed off look, Gunn says, 'Wot you doing?'

Cadija folds her arms. 'Listen, yeah, I've been here for over one hour, and you haven't said but two words to me.'

Gunn grits his teeth. 'I told you to wait, yeah? I'm in here praying.'

'What, for over an hour?'

Gunn picks up his Koran. 'Don't watch how long it takes me to pray, respec' sutum, man.'

Cadija licks her lips. 'Yeah but, babes, I'm feeling neglected. Look, you didn't even notice my new hair style and nails.' Cadija had sat in the hairdresser for almost eight hours getting her hair and nails done, for the pleasure of her boyfriend.

Gunn kisses his teeth. 'Dat's why if you was a sister, you wouldn't be so superficial and you would know your place, inshallah.'

'What do you mean my place, like I'm some dog or something?' Cadija puts her hand onto her hip awaiting Gunn's answer. In reality this is what turns Cadija on, from the moment she met Gunn; he never showed that her stunning beauty ever fazed him. He always treats her like it is nothing to be with her and always gives it to her doggy style.

'Huh,' says Gunn, and sits down on his bed. 'You listening? I'm gonna read my Koran, you do wot you're doing.'

'So what, you don't care if I go to a wine bar with Tracey and the girls?'

Without looking at his wifey, Gunn replies, 'I don't care wot you do or where you go, just leave my presence.' Gunn flicks his finger towards Cadija. A lump rises in her throat. She holds back tears and moves slowly from the door disappearing from Gunn's presence.

Gunn opens his Koran and begins reading; deep down he had hoped to convert her to Islam and marry her. He huffs at the thought, then gets up to shut his door as his phone rings.

Chapter Twenty-Seven

There is a long line of people waiting to go into Satay Bar; inside is almost ram. Paro, Thomas and the three other men occupy the seating area near the doors.

Paro leans forward to Thomas and the other men. 'Ahm telling you, you know, rudeboy—' He takes a sip of his champagne. '—shoting on da block is long. It's not like da old days, d'you get me, rudeboy?' Paro takes another sip. 'First of all da dutty Boy-Dem has cameras everywhere, d'you get me, rudeboy? Dey don't even have to send undercovers again to take pictures of man.' Paro sucks on his teeth. ''R rassclart pictures are being taken twenty-four-seven, d'you get me, rudeboy?'

Paro reaches out to hit fists with Thomas but before their fists can connect one of the other men shouts: 'Jheez, look at dem tings.'

Thomas, Paro and the other men lock their eyes onto Cadija and her friends as they swoop into Satay Bar.

Paro knows Cadija's friend, Tracey, who was once a hardcore Brixton girl that bit out a piece of a girl's face she was fighting with, but after a stint in prison she has now calmed down. Paro calls her over. She smiles, grips Cadija by the arm and steps over to Paro with the other friends following in tow.

Paro stands up and greets Tracey with a kiss, then says, 'Who's your friends...?' Pausing to control himself from saying rudeboy.

Tracey shouts, 'Oh this is Cadija—' she pulls Cadija closer to her '—and this Akua and Mya.'

Cadija, Akua and Mya smile as Paro shakes their hands.

Bassy Hip-Hop music pumps around the small space of Satay Bar. Paro smiles and says just about loud enough, 'Yeah, and dis is da man-dem.' He turns and gestures to Thomas and the other three men. The men all smile and give a quick nod. Paro motions for the girls to sit. The guys make room for them.

Cadija, sits next to Thomas. It doesn't take a second for him to begin spitting game into Gunn's wifey's ear. Cadija is feeling what Thomas is saying as Paro lays out more glasses for the girls and pours some champagne.

Chapter Twenty-Eight

Gunn steps out of his house dressed in blue with a man-bag strapped across his shoulder. He makes his way over to a silver car with tinted windows. Before he gets into the car, Gunn readjusts the man-bag.

'Assalamu alaikum,' he says as he closes the car door. He is hit with the scent of brand-new leather seats.

His Muslim brothers return the ancient Islamic greeting.

The driver, whose name is Driver—because at the age of ten, he was already stealing cars from housing estates and driving them—turns down the music so everyone can be heard.

'So, wot you saying, ak?' Gunn says to Driver. 'We're gonna turn over Satay Bar?'

Driver smiles. 'Inshallah, akhi, inshallah.'

Driver picks out five balaclavas from the door pockets. 'Eya,' he says and hands out the balaclavas to Gunn and three other Muslim brothers who are sitting quiet in the back of the car. They have been recently converted to Islam through fear. This will be their first experience of the awesome, forceful power that an individual can wield once they have faith in Allah.

Gunn glances out of the tinted windows, then dips into his man-bag and pulls out his gun.

'Listen,' he says, 'we ain't on no long ting. It's just an in-and-out ting. We're just gonna peel dese kuffars and blow, Inshallah.'

Gunn's Muslim brothers nod, and repeat, 'Inshallah.'

Gunn looks at Driver. 'Akhi, you know wot to do, yeah?'

'Course,' Driver says.

Gunn loads his gun. 'OK,' he says, 'so da moment we take out da security—' Gunn glances behind at the other Muslim brothers in the back of the car '—me and da akhis are gonna roll up in dere. Dat's when you lock off da door from outside, den it's bang-bang, peel dem.'

Driver starts the car, nodding in agreement. 'Inshallah. Allahu Akbar.'

Gunn puts his gun back into his man-bag, as Driver swerves off from the kerb, leaving smoke from his burning tyres behind him.

Chapter Twenty-Nine

There is still a queue outside Satay Bar; most of the wannabe patrons won't get in tonight. Inside, Thomas has his arm around Gunn's wifey. She is leaning into him and laughing as he runs joke into her ear. Smoothly, he caresses her thigh. Suddenly Cadija's eyes widen as she realises she's making herself slip. Cadija reaches for her glass of champagne, takes a sip, and with the most pleasant smile she can manage, tells Thomas she'll be back in a moment. Cadija grabs Tracey's hand and makes her way to the toilets.

Inside the disinfectant and bleach smelling toilets, Tracey laughs, then says, 'You little tart, what will Gunn say?'

Cadija does not answer and moves over to the mirror.

Tracey says, 'Nah, but for real, Gunn's a waste man. He used to be the shits but since this Muslim ting he's become a waste man. He doesn't even hustle all he does is rob and lick man down.' Tracey goes into her purse and takes out her lip-gloss; she looks into the mirror as she applies it. 'For real, you don't need no man like that.'

'I know, babes,' Cadija says, 'but I love him. It's not that easy, and underneath all that thug shit he's a nice sweet person.' Cadija takes out her hairbrush from the female version of Gunn's man-bag and brushes her long jet-black hair.

Tracey turns away from the mirror and looks at Cadija. 'Look at you, look how beautiful you are, you're wasting your self on that waste man. I know you love him but you can have any man you want, you don't have to take his shit.'

Cadija does not respond. She stops brushing her hair.

Tracey continues. 'You've got that nice sexy Yardie out there feeling you but you're too hung up on that chauvinistic bastard to do anything about it.' Tracey puts her lip-gloss back into her purse. 'Well if you're not gonna take that Yardie, I will.'

Cadija turns away from the mirror. 'Be easy, babes. You're going to have to find your own sexy Yardie.'

Tracey blurts out laughing followed by Cadija.

As they exit the toilet, Gunn approaches Satay Bar.

Chapter Thirty

The silver tinted car passes Satay Bar and stops outside the traffic lights on the junction of Coldharbour Lane, Brixton Road, and Acre Lane.

Gunn says, 'Oi, Driver, dat's Satay Bar back dere, you know. It's better we park on da corner just before da bar.'

Driver shakes his head. 'Nah, ak not dat bar. I'm always getting the bars mixed up.' Driver motions towards Acre Lane. 'I meant dis bar up dere, man.'

Gunn looks at Driver. 'Naam, Z Bar, yeah?'

'Yeah, Z Bar, Naam' he replies. 'Satay Bar is owned by brudders.'

Driver takes his foot off the brake and drives past the traffic lights.

Gunn taps his man-bag. 'Naam, Satay Bar is owned by akhis, yeah? A'ight, well it's Z Bar.' Gunn rubs his hands together. 'Remember, it's da same ting; nufin' long, in-and-out. Inshallah.'

Driver is about to move into the path, which will take him up to Acre Lane.

Gunn says, 'Nah, listen, go straight and go around

onto Trinity Gardens. Den park at da back.'

Driver heads in the direction instructed. Moments later, he stops and parks on the corner of Trinity Gardens. He shuts off the engine.

Gunn gives everyone a final command: 'No love for da faithless, alhamdulillah.'

Everyone pops their doors and jump out the car. Gunn leads them to Z Bar, while over at Satay Bar his wifey gives her number to Thomas.

Chapter Thirty-One

Z Bar has a peaceful vibe running through it. Mellow music flows through the speakers. An assortment of great tasting food permeates a sweet aroma throughout the wine bar.

The man with the pretty flat nose sits at the back of the bar at his usual table, eating food with his date, when he hears the music abruptly stop. Then someone screams.

Gunn rolls into the bar with his 9mm in hand. Two beefy security men are pushed in behind him while holding their faces as blood seeps from between their fingers.

The house lights come on. Everyone is silent until Gunn lets off two shots towards the ceiling. A high-pitched scream splits the air. The pretty flat nose man looks towards the scream; he grits his teeth and flares his nose. Gunn's voice bellows: 'Mashallah! We're 'ere to rob you.'

The patrons on the dance floor spread, making way for Gunn. With his 9mm held out, he bops through the crowd.

One of the Muslim brothers that sat in the back of the car keeps guard of the two beefy securities while the other two walk through the crowd. They poke their guns in the faces of two guys wearing gold chains. Without even talking, they get the men to take off their chains.

The Muslim brothers smile, pocket the chains, and peel others at random.

Gunn has the club manager in a tight grip by a small safe under the bar. He whispers in his ear, 'You got a minute to open da safe or it will be da last minute you breathe.'

The club manager squirms and, quick as a lightning strike destroys a tall tree, pops open the safe door. Gunn scrapes out the money, whilst his accomplices work their way up the bar, taking belongings which do not belong to them.

The man with the pretty flat nose feels his stomach twist again but it's not out of fear. He has the kill-or-be-killed rage seeping through him. There is no way he is going to allow these hurry-come-ups to rob him; he has lived in Brixton, and was on road, all his adolescent life and has never been robbed. And he won't be now. He grips his steak knife as Gunn's Muslim brothers approach his table. His date clutches his other hand. His eyes connect with them; they seem to pause for a millisecond as if they see the fearless rage in his eyes. They raise their tools of destruction, but before they can utter any words, Gunn shouts, 'OK, we're done here. Let's go!'

Like automatic reacting robots, Gunn's Muslim

brothers turn away from the man and head towards the exit.

The pretty flat nose man loosens his grip on the steak knife as he watches Gunn and his followers stroll out of the bar with a loot of thirty one thousand pounds.

Chapter Thirty-Two

As Gunn and his followers make their way to their getaway car, Gunn is overcome by a feeling of conscience. A verse in the Koran hits him and makes him realise robbing non-Muslims, or anyone for that matter, is haraam, which means it is not allowed and wrong—dead wrong. Gunn shrugs off the feeling and dials his girlfriend. He can't get through, but then gets a call from a girl that he's been sexing on and off for over a year. Unknowingly to Gunn, the girl wants him to become her man. He decides to crash at her house until any heat from the robbery blows over. Him and his followers make it to the car without anyone from the bar looking to see which direction they had gone.

The pretty flat nose man hasn't moved from his seat either, but not out of fear; he just doesn't want to know which direction they've gone. He releases the knife completely from his hand as he hears distant sirens raging towards the bar. He grabs his date by the wrist and steps to the exit. He is met by scrolls of shocked-looking people, with expressions that suggest they're asking *why?* He thinks to himself: *they should ask a dif-*

ferent question—what? What could make these yutes turn from cute, helpless little babies into destructive terrorizing young adults? Young adults who callously leave shocked victims behind, and sometimes victims who will never see day turn to night again, leaving the nights filled with wailing blue sirens.

He has now reached his car, and the sirens he heard from inside the bar are much louder as police cars zoom past him. The barrage of police vehicles screech to a halt outside Z Bar. He gets into and starts his car, then swerves out of the tight parking space. He breaks suddenly as a police car stops in front of him. His body falls weak, not from believing that the police car purposely blocked him in, but because he thought he saw a face that he hadn't seen for almost fifteen years.

The face of a police officer everyone called John Wayne because of his bravado ways. Back in the eighties John Wayne was sent along with his partner, The Runner to get rid of all the purse-snatching criminals in Brixton. Then in the nineties John Wayne was sent again to get rid of the Yardie gangs. Whenever John Wayne rolled up on the block everyone would scatter, or those who moved too late would be caught in John Wayne's web, which was not a nice place to be because you could find yourself charged for being in possession of a weapon, or drugs, that didn't belong to you.

The police car reverses away and the officer jumps out. The pretty flat nose man's heart rate falls back to normal as he realises it's not John Wayne. He releases the break and drives off into the night.

The Following Day

Brixton:
Stockwell Park Estate

Chapter Thirty-Three

The day begins quiet on Stockwell Park Estate. It usually starts like this, even after the days when "Da Boy-Dem" moved everyone who lived on Somerleyton Road—a road that housed most of the Jamaican immigrants—to the brand new housing estate which lies in between Stockwell Park Road and Brixton Road. But as the days dragged on and dragged hundreds of victims of circumstance out of bed, the estate would become a haven from the police and allowed countless robberies, shoting, even murder and rape. This bright sunny cold day will draw another black cloud over Stockwell Park as a murder once again echoes out of the estate and onto the streets and into the media.

Armed police have their sub-machine guns aimed at their target.

'Put down your weapon... Armed police!' shouts the leading officer.

Dunkley, the suspect, who has just been robbed at gunpoint and beaten down gets up from the floor holding a reactivated handgun. The gun was used to rob him but the robbers carelessly dropped it as they made their getaway.

He says, 'This is not my gun… I've been trying to tell you, the bastards used this to rob me.' The suspect stumbles back as blood trickles down his face.

The leading officer shouts again, 'This is your final warning, put down your weapon and get down on your knees.'

The suspect stumbles forward bringing the gun shoulder high and says, 'Aren't you lot listening…?'

His words are cut short as bullets burst through his defenseless body and bring him to his knees. He kneels stiffly for a moment, hand tightly gripping the gun. His eyes shut and his body sharply meets the rubber landing.

That night the national newspapers would write a story in favour of the police just because the suspect had a criminal record of being a drug dealer, rather than reporting the actual facts, which were: *The suspect, known as Devon Brown, who was robbed by teenage kids using a reactivated handgun for his hard earned money that he worked twelve hours a day for inside a mail sorting warehouse where he had been employed for the last ten years, was gunned down today by trigger-happy police.*

Instead it read: *Known Stockwell Park drug dealer and Ex-Raiders gang member, Devon Brown, finally got his comeuppance as he faced off with armed police in Stockwell Park Estate and was brought to his knees in a fierce bloody shoot out.*

Two Days Later

Chapter Thirty-Four

Brixton Road is busy as usual. The police station doors have been open all night to the public. At present it is filled with people waiting to sign their names in a book, which tells the courts they're still in the country and have not skipped bail.

Upstairs in a large conference room that is suffused with the stench of coffee and new leather, sits Lambeth's Borough Commander, two officials from Scotland Yard—which isn't actually in Scotland—and Detective Chief Inspector Moore—who is about to retire in a few days—along with a fresh face officer, Jack Mills, who helped to shoot and kill Devon Brown.

The Borough Commander looks at the two officers and says, 'I must say, I am very disappointed in the operation that took place at the weekend.'

DCI Moore raises his hand. 'To be fair, Marm, we had no choice.' DCI Moore looks at the fresh face officer. 'The suspect pointed a gun at us.'

The Borough Commander crosses her fingers together. 'That is understandable, but we are trying to stop death by guns in the black community, not add to it...'

DCI Moore butts in: 'Doing our job can hardly constitute as adding to black-on-black gun crime and, Marm, it is not only black areas suffering from gun crime. There are many white areas in England suffering as well, and hardly anything is being done to tackle the problem in those areas.'

The Borough Commander looks down at the black file in front of her. 'Nevertheless,' she says as she looks back up at DCI Moore, 'certain groups feel that you and your men reacted too soon and could have avoided killing a hardworking citizen.'

DCI Moore's brow wrinkles up. 'Marm, this piece of work sold drugs to children and was part of the notorious Raiders gang, so who knows what more destruction he caused back then.'

The Borough Commander flips over the cover of Devon Brown's file. 'Inspector, you damn well know Mr Brown's conviction was over fifteen years ago and his gang member days ended over twenty years ago.'

DCI Moore makes no reply. He looks to the ground then back at the Borough Commander. She introduces the two Scotland Yard officials. 'This is Mr Scott and Mr Barnes from Scotland Yard. They have been sent to monitor and oversee all future operations of your Special Armed Trident Unit.'

The officers acknowledge the officials with nods.

Mr Scott clears his throat and straightens his tie. 'Thank you,' he says, looking at the Borough Commander. He returns his attention back onto DCI Moore and Jack. 'Your men were very lucky that the

Press was on our side this time. We cannot afford to suffer any more embarrassment with our policing. Be assured the time will come when someone will have to take the fall. In light of this, we are taking precautions by sending for support to help with your Special Trident Armed Unit.'

Mr Barnes hands Mr Scott a file. 'A highly decorated officer—' Mr Scott opens the file '—now based in Kingston, Jamaica, will lend his expertise at gun crime. He will command the Special Armed Unit and replace you—' Mr Scott looks at DCI Moore '—after you retire.'

Mr Scott closes the file on John Wayne, a bent copper who was sent back in the day, along with another, to catch purse-snatching criminals. An officer that chased a suspect from the bottom of Acre Lane all the way to Clapham Common tube station where he finally caught the suspect; and from that day on the man-dem called him "Da Runner". Da Runner caused the purse snatchers to change their hustle. That is when John Wayne became bent. He used to roll up on the block by himself, making the man-dem scatter. The ones who were not quick enough, he would interrogate and plant knives or drugs on them. He then would threaten to bring them to the station if they didn't give him information. He would then force these informers to sell drugs for him.

Eventually John Wayne was caught, but because the informers refused to give evidence against him, he was merely transferred out of Brixton Police Station to Kingston, Jamaica.

Kingston: Jamaica
48 Hours Later

Chapter Thirty-Five

John Wayne rolls up his shirtsleeves, pulls off his tie and undoes four top buttons. He sits down in his cool air-conditioned office as the hot sun beats at his window, which overlooks the ghetto of Kingston. His six-foot-seven inch frame fills out the chair as he flicks through the pages of a pornographic Internet site called, "Big Black Butts".

John Wayne looks up as his phone rings. He answers. 'Chief Inspector Wain.'

John Wayne closes down the Internet sex page. 'Pardon,' he says as he raises his eyebrows and runs his fingers in his wavy blonde hair that has fine streaks of grey running through it. 'OK… OK. How soon do you want me on a plane?' John Wayne's eyes widen. 'Tonight? Surely it cannot be that urgent…?'

The voice on the other end of the phone replies, 'I'm afraid it is. You were meant to be at Scotland Yard six hours ago but due to an administration cock up…'

John Wayne gets up from his seat. 'I understand. What time is my flight?'

'22.15, your time. Kingston Tinson Airport.'

John Wayne hangs up the phone and, before he knows it, is on a private jet flying away from the little island of Jamaica, which has been his home for the past ten years and where he helped to worsen the crime rate on the streets of Kingston, and fathered eight children from six different Jamaican women.

It won't be long until John Wayne worsens the crime rate on the streets of Brixton and fathers a few more children.

Brixton: London
24 Hours Later

Chapter Thirty-Six

With no moon or stars in the sky, the night has fallen dark on Coldharbour Lane, Brixton's new "Frontline". Only the lights from the open shops and street lamps illuminate the black faces that stand in the cold, waiting for business in the form of crack heads and weed heads. A crack head rolls up to the cab station to get a shot; she's about five foot two with a face full of spots, cuts and bruises. Back in the day she was pretty as heaven but her prettiness has now vanished from years of drug, alcohol and sex abuse. She's about to reach her shotter when two men on a motorbike that seems to come out of nowhere pulls up beside her. The person on the back of the bike removes a Mac-10 machine pistol. He opens fire, emptying thirty rounds of ammunition in 1.57 seconds. Before the first second could tick over everyone outside the cab station hits the ground. The gunman takes out a new magazine but before he can load it an undercover police car with siren blazing screeches to a halt.

The motorbike rider roars the bike into a wheelie. John Wayne's six-foot-seven inch frame jumps out of the car. He opens fire. The motorbike rider speeds off down the road making the gunman on the back drop the new magazine.

Chapter Thirty-Seven

John Wayne picks up the magazine, puts it in his pocket, and then sticks his gun into its holster. He calls in the incident, which destroyed the windows of the cab station and the adjacent shops but left no victims. The people who had hit the ground are now on their feet. As they scatter some swallow the crack they had to sell.

'Come here!' John Wayne demands. 'Where do you think you're going, fella?'

The five-foot-two crack head freezes. John Wayne pulls towards him a tall young man who is almost the same height as him and then looks at the five foot two crack head. 'No, not you, be on your way.'

She doesn't move.

'Now!' shouts John Wayne.

With her little legs, and dirty five-sizes-too-big shoes, she shuffles off quickly as possible.

'Now, you, stand up there.' John Wayne pushes the tall young man up against a wall. 'Right, you're going to tell me what happened out here tonight.'

'I swear down, I don't know nufin'. I just came back

down from Birmingham tonight, man.'

John Wayne grips the tall young man by his long neck. 'You're going to tell me something or you will never see the road again, and I don't mean because you'll be behind bars.'

If outside wasn't so cold the tall young man would have a bead of sweat from fear running down the side of his face. He says, 'Well, at least handcuff me den, so it don't look like I'm going to da station to snitch.'

John Wayne handcuffs the young man, sticks him in his car and drives off into the night as a brigade of officers' swamp onto "Frontline".

Chapter Thirty-Eight

John Wayne pushes open the interview room door, bringing the tall young man into view. He is sitting on a blue chair behind a small grey table; another blue chair is opposite him. The tall young man is nervously rubbing his hands together as John Wayne steps into the room and closes the door behind him. He pulls out the other blue chair from under the table and sits. John Wayne pulls out his phone, takes out the battery, then calmly says, 'Talk.'

The tall young man rubs the corners of his mouth. 'You're not gonna tape me, are you?'

John Wayne leans back in his chair. 'No… Anything said in this room stays in this room.'

With paranoia in his eyes, the tall young man looks to his right then his left. 'OK, OK,' he says, 'da shooting tonight was done by a crew dat's running Brixton—da Muslim brudders. Dey call demselves Akhis. Dey're robbing and even killing anyone and everyone who are not Muslims.' The tall young man swallows hard. 'I'm not even religious but have become a Muslim so I don't get robbed or killed.'

John Wayne takes out a pen and notepad and jots down some notes. 'What about the armed robbery at Stockwell Park?'

The tall young man nods. 'Yeah, it was dem.'

'And the robbery at that winebar.'

'Dem too.'

'So who is leading these Muslim Boys?'

The tall young man wipes the corners of his mouth again. 'Gunn...some boy called Gunn. He built da Peel Dem Crew dat came out of da younger, younger, younger 28s.'

John Wayne adds to his notepad. 'Oh, the 28s. I remember them bastards. So they're not around no longer?'

'Nah...not really," answers the tall young man. "Dere's no more 28s, it's just dese boys wid big guns and no brains.'

'Mmm...' John Wayne adds to his notepad. 'So where can I find this Gunn and his mates?'

The tall young man looks in John Wayne's eyes. 'Baghdad... Sorry, I mean Myatts Fields.'

6:00 A.M.
Monday Morning
Police Brief Meeting

Chapter Thirty-Nine

'Myatts Fields,' says John Wayne as he finishes writing Myatts Fields on a white board. He circles it. "Myatts Fields North, that is, not south.' He turns around to face a room full of officers. 'Myatts Fields, Brixton.' John Wayne throws the blue marker on a table. 'Which they now affectionately call Baghdad.'

The officers bust out laughing.

John Wayne says, 'Charming, ha?' and moves over to the front of the table and sits on the edge. 'Now make no mistake, Myatts Fields has always been a shit-hole but for it to be now called Baghdad it must really have gone to the dogs.' John Wayne clears his throat. 'And going to the dogs is an understatement. Now, according to my informant, a group called The Muslim Boys who congregate in Myatts Fields, were behind the armed robbery at Stockwell Park and at the wine bar. Reportedly they are also responsible for eighty-percent of all murders throughout the capital.'

John Wayne takes the cup of coffee, which has just been brought into him, and sips. 'But due to the fear of reprisals, no informant has yet been willing to testify against The Muslim Boys in Court. I am optimistic this will change.'

Jack, the fresh face officer who helped shoot and kill Devon Brown in Stockwell Park Estate and who has recently been made detective, raises his hand. 'What do you think will bring about this change, Sir?'

John Wayne rubs his lips together. 'Good question. I'll be employing a new technique in Covert Human Intelligence Sources. I believe along with surveillance, and my informant, we will be able to bring our target…' John Wayne turns around and picks up a picture from the table '…the leader of the Muslim Boys, a one Mr. Jerome Boor, also known as Gunn, to prosecution.' John Wayne hands Gunn's photo to the officers. 'And according to my informant he has been hiding out, after the robbery at the wine bar, in a property over in Myatts Fields South, St Lawrence Way.'

Chapter Forty

Gunn wakes in a one bedroom flat in St Lawrence Way, Myatts Fields South. The flat belongs to a girl named Leandra who believes she has now become Gunn's wifey.

Leandra steps into the messy bedroom with breakfast on a tray. 'Morning, babes...are you awake? I've got you breakfast.'

Gunn raises his head and is met by the smell of eggs on burnt toast. 'Wot have I told you? I don't eat breakfast in da morning.' Gunn sucks his teeth. 'And every morning you try bring me breakfast. Wot's wrong wid you?' Gunn sucks his teeth again. Leandra leaves the room.

Before Gunn came to stay at Leandra's house he thought she was a girl that kept her house tidy. But living in the house for a week he realised that she must have always tidied up just before he came because Gunn feels he has been waking up in a dump, and this is the reason why he does not eat breakfast from her in the mornings. Instead, Gunn has been waiting until she leaves for work, then gets one of his youngers to bring him a big breakfast, without the pork.

Gunn's phone rings. He answers it, but doesn't speak.

'Assalamu alaikum,' says a voice.

Gunn sits up a bit. 'Assalamu alaikum, wah gwan, wa rahmatullah?'

A man's high pitch voice comes through the phone. 'Hey, wot's going on, B? Where you at?'

'I'm still on da ends init, ak. Why, wot's wrong?'

'Nah, nuttin', I'm just checking if you still remember bout da ting we gotah do today?'

Gunn closes his eyes. His hustle never ends. He kicks his legs out of the bed and opens his eyes. 'Yeah, akhi, man, wot's wrong wid you? I'm just gonna get up out of dis wastechick's yard, in a minute.'

The bedroom door opens. Gunn looks at Leandra, thinking whether she overheard him or not. He sucks on his teeth. He doesn't care if she did. Gunn promptly ends the call. Leandra moves over to her wardrobe and starts digging through the piles of shoes she has stacked in between her clothes. She finds the pair she wants to wear, then turns and faces Gunn. 'I don't know how you do it. Start da day widout no breakfast.'

Gunn doesn't reply as he looks away from Leandra and leans back onto the headboard. Leandra puts on the right foot of her shoe. 'Because all I wanna do is take care of my man and feed him breakfast.'

Gunn sharply turns his head towards Leandra. 'Wot? Oi, don't get it twisted, I'm not your man.'

Leandra puts on the other foot of her shoe. 'So, wot has dis whole week been about?'

Gunn screws his face. 'Wot do you mean? Wot, just because I've been here banging you don't make me your man. 'R you dumb?'

Leandra picks up her bag. 'I really don't want dis conversation. I got to go to work. We'll talk bout dis later.'

Gunn doesn't reply. He'll be leaving her house after he eats his big breakfast and will never return.

Six Hours Later

Chapter Forty-One

Leandra's front door opens. Gunn steps out dressed in black with a manbag strapped over his shoulder. Opposite, in a blacked out space cruiser, sits John Wayne and his team of surveillance officers. An officer with a large head and red rings around his neck takes pictures of Gunn. Unaware, Gunn stands perfectly still as he waits for his ride while the camera snaps at him.

Gunn moves his head to the right...

Snap.

Gunn moves his head to the left...

Snap.

Gunn moves his head back to the middle...

Snap.

Gunn readjusts his manbag...

Snap.

Gunn's ride pulls up...

Snap.

Gunn opens the door to get in...

Snap.

Gunn gets into the silver car...

Snap.

The silver car drives off…

Snap.

The officer with the large head lowers the camera. 'Got 'em, Chief.'

John Wayne looks at the driver. 'Drive.'

The driver smoothly pulls out of the parking space and follows Gunn.

The officer with the large head turns to the fresh face officer Jack and says, 'He doesn't look like much.'

'Yeah,' Jack replies. 'He looks like a piece of piss.'

John Wayne says, 'First rule in dealing with these animals, never underestimate them.' John Wayne licks his lips. 'Yeah, he looks like a piece of piss but him holding a gun and you trying to arrest him might have you pissing your fucking pants as he puts a bullet in your fucking bladder.'

Jack says, 'OK, Chief, you made your point.'

John Wayne taps the steering wheel and says to the driver, 'Slow down a bit.'

The driver eases off the speed as the car that Gunn is in slows down then stops at a large traffic light junction.

Chapter Forty-Two

The silver car that Gunn is in remains stationary at the traffic lights. Inside, Gunn is sitting in the passenger seat and Driver is driving as usual. In the back sits a tall young man with a long skinny neck, which resembles a snake, who is called Najash. He has been up in Birmingham, a city that is 112 miles away from London, for the past six months causing mayhem. He is now back in Brixton and has already convinced Gunn to take set on Thomas's cousin, Redy.

Najash taps Gunn's shoulder. 'Oi, akhi, you listening?'

The traffic lights turn green. Driver puts the car into first gear and cruises it down the road.

Najash says, 'You know dis yute really thinks he's gonna buss and not make da akhis eat.' Najash rises in his seat. 'Can you believe dat? Naam, he's taking dis for a game, ak. He's taking dis for a joke, gang.'

Gunn's lips press together and his nose flares. 'So, wot, he's mashing ber pees, yeah?'

'Naam, ber pees, cuz, and going on like he's too bad for da world to break sutum off.'

Driver shakes his head. 'Redy's taking da piss, star. Dem man der is taking liberties.'

Najash eyes widen. 'You dun know, init, Driver, ber liberties. We shouldn't even talk and just bun him, inshallah.'

Gunn looks out of the window. 'Mashallah, but let's hear wot he's saying first.'

Najash rubs his nose. 'Akhi, you don't understand, I think talking to dis yute is long, I wanna bun him, bad.' Najash squeezes his right hand together in a tight fist. 'Because when I told him he had to convert to Islam, he's telling me some shit bout he was born a Christian and will die a Christian, astaghfirullah.' Najash shakes his head. 'I'm telling you we should get jihad on him and leave him faceless for being faithless.'

With wisdom beaming from his eyes, Gunn calmly says, 'Akhi, just cool. Inshallah.'

Which means if God willed it then Redy will get killed for being faithless.

Chapter Forty-Three

Redy slouches on the sofa he's been sitting on for the past hour, smoking weed with Thomas and Paro. Thomas and Paro are second cousins to Redy, which also makes Redy, without knowing, a distant cousin to Gunn. Thomas has been staying in Redy's house since he came from Jamaica.

Redy's phone rings. He answers. 'Yeah, who's dat?'

Over the loudspeaker, the voice says, 'It's me, babes, Sherene.'

'Ah, wah gwan, B?'

'Nuttin'… so wot, sweetie, are we still linking today?'

Redy sits up in the chair. 'Yeah, oh yeah.'

'Wot, did you forget bout me, babes?' Sherene asks.

Redy looks at Thomas and Paro; he raises his eyebrows. 'Nah, how am I gonna forget a sweet ting like you? I'm just 'ere buning some weed wid da man-dem, init.'

Sherene's voice is crackled as it comes through the loudspeaker.

'Wot?' Redy says. 'Say dat again.'

'I said I got something real special to give you today… I'm sure you're gonna love it like last time.'

Redy clears his throat. 'Yeah? A'ight give me until tonight and I'll come and check you, init.'

With distress in her voice, Sherene states, 'Nah, babes, can't you come now because my man wants to take me out tonight?'

Redy hesitates, then says, 'OK, I'll see wot I can do, I'll see you soon.'

Redy ends the call and looks over at Thomas and Paro. 'Dese flipping chicks, man. Always bawling for da cocky.' He gets up from the sofa and stretches. 'Cha, I don't even wanna go, but her pussy's good.'

Thomas and Paro laugh. Thomas says, 'Mine yuh mek pussy kill yuh.'

Redy smiles. 'Better dat, better pussy kill me yes.'

Everyone laughs. Redy hits Thomas and Paro's fist with his. 'A'ight blud, I'll be back in awhile, just gonna mash up and kill some pussy.'

Thomas and Paro nod at Redy as he steps away from them and out of his bedroom door.

Chapter Forty-Four

Sherene locks off her phone and looks at Najash. 'He's coming.'

'Wot, are you sure?'

Sherene puts her phone in her pocket. 'Yeah, he's coming now.'

'Where's he coming to?'

'Here, init, my house.' Sherene gestures towards her front door.

'Wot, is he rolling by himself?'

Sherene licks her lips. 'Yeah, he must be. Wot, can I go now?'

'Nah, not until he rolls up, den you can go.'

Sherene tuts. 'But he's gonna be awhile.'

'So wot!'

Sherene folds her arms and looks out of the window. 'But I've got something to do in my house, man.'

A cold expression slides over Najash's face. 'Oi, you must want me to slap you to death. I don't care how long he takes, you're waiting here until he comes.'

Sherene kisses her teeth and looks into the direction of Gunn who is sitting silently holding his black 9mm

Glock.

Twenty minutes pass, and Redy pulls into Cowley Estate that is off Brixton Road and which was built by the London County Council in the 1930s.

Redy drives past the car which John Wayne and his "Merry Men" are sitting in then drives past the car which has Gunn and his "Merry Men" waiting in.

Sherene points. 'Dere he is.'

'Where?'

Everyone looks as Redy finds a space to park his car.

'Dere, parking his car,' Sherene says. 'Can I go now please?'

'A'ight, go.'

Sherene jumps out of the car and runs to her front door. Moments later Redy gets out of his car and walks back to Sherene's house.

Redy freezes in his stride as he becomes parallel with Gunn's car. His facial muscles tighten up like hooks are pulling his skin back. He realises what is about to go down. His feet feel glued to the floor. The car doors pop open and Gunn, followed by Najash, jump out. They grip Redy by the arms and frog march him away past John Wayne and his "Merry Men."

Chapter Forty-Five

Redy is pushed through a gap in a fence that used to secure Mostyn Adventure Playground, a playground in Mostyn Gardens, Myatts Fields that has been closed since the late 90s. Mostyn Adventure Playground is now nothing more than a derelict wasteland with a boarded up hut and abandoned vehicles sitting outside in the middle of Mostyn Gardens' hilly green grass area, a perfect place to bring harm to someone far from preying eyes.

Najash pokes Redy in the side of his head and makes him fall back against the dirty green wall of the boarded up hut. 'Oi, fam, so ain't it true you've been going on and chatting like you're greasy, like you don't want da akhis to eat?'

Redy straightens his head. 'Wot do you mean? I ain't been talking greasy.'

Najash pokes Redy in the side of the head again; this time a bit harder and with two fingers. 'Hey, don't stand up here and lie, you know.' Najash bites his lip as a vein in his neck starts to throb. He's about to explode his full rage on Redy when Gunn taps his knuckles into his distant cousin's chest.

'Oi, you listening? My brudder.' Gunn looks at Najash, who is only his brother by faith, then back at Redy. 'He's telling me dat now dat you've bust, you're going on like you don't wanna break off nuttin' for da brudders.'

'Dat's a lie,' Redy cuts in. 'I don't know who's been saying dat but dat's a lie. I swear down, I swear on da Holy Bible.'

Calmly, Gunn says, 'Forget bout dat, cos dat's da talk on road.' The right corner of Gunn's top lip rises and wrinkles up the scar he has beside his nostril. 'And we can't have dat, can we?'

Redy swallows hard. 'A'ight, give me a few weeks, and I'll drop some pees on you.'

Gunn is going to accept these terms, because for some reason that he cannot explain, he kind of likes Redy, until Najash jumps in and says, 'Nah, gee. Wot are you talking about a few weeks?' Najash points two of his boney fingers towards his feet. 'You gotah drop some pees by tomorrow. Inshallah.'

Gunn laughs to himself and looks towards the muddy ground.

Redy's eyes become full of rage; his pupils shrink. 'Listen, I can't get no pees to you by tomorrow.'

Najash shakes his head. 'I don't wanna hear dat, because if we ain't getting some pees by tomorrow it's better you say we're not getting no pees at all.'

Anger fills Redy's voice. 'OK, den, you're not getting no pees at all den.'

That is the last sentence Redy will ever say because

without warning Najash pulls out his gun and sends five bullets to his head.

Chapter Forty-Six

As the third bullet goes into Redy's skull, quickly followed by the fourth and fifth. Jack shouts, 'Holy shit!' then unclips his gun and pops open the car door.

Before he can jump out, John Wayne grips hold of his arm. 'Where do you think you're going?'

Jack looks at him as if to say, is it not obvious? 'Did you not just see what bloody happened?' he says frantically.

'Close the door,' John Wayne growls.

It takes a moment for Jack to react; his heart is pounding as he watches Gunn and Najash running away from Redy's body.

John Wayne repeats, 'Jack, close the door.'

Jack finally closes the door; his eyes are wide, body shaking. He lets go of his gun and looks at the large head officer who has the camera on his lap. 'I cannot believe what just happened. Did you get shots of what just happened?'

The large head officer doesn't reply. John Wayne turns to Jack. 'Calm down, Jack, this is just part of my new technique, which ironically is the lifeline of our job.'

Jack rubs his head. 'How cannot reacting to what just happened be the lifeline of our job? We just witnessed a man being murdered and did nothing.'

'Jack, my boy,' John Wayne says with a hint of joy in his voice, 'the lifeline of our job is maintaining our job. What just happened maintains our job.' John Wayne cocks his right eye at Jack. 'Listen, if these black bastards stop doing crime tomorrow we would not have a job.' John Wayne waves his finger towards where Redy lies dead. 'Don't you understand we need these cunts to rise crime so that the system can have the excuse to raise taxes and also introduce new legislation to slowly take away the Nation's liberties?'

Jack's breathing slows down.

John Wayne continues. 'Jack, do not worry, son. These animals mainly kill each other.' He raises his hands to his ears. 'OK, fair enough, maybe now and again an innocent person gets caught in the crossfire but we all have to make sacrifices for a higher cause.'

Jack, with somber eyes, slowly nods. 'I understand,' he says as the memory of him helping to shoot Devon Brown to death impedes his mind.

'I'm glad you understand, Jack, and try not to feel too bad because the root cause of knife crime, gun crime and gang culture is a combination of these black bastards' destructive mentality and ignorance.' John Wayne looks at Jack to check if he is taking heed. 'The system only manipulates this a little; granted, the system could be honest and educate them how powerful their minds can be, but if it did there would be no need to make drugs or guns illegal, thus destroying the underground black markets, which is at the essence of our operations.' John Wayne clears his throat. 'This cycle must continue…as I have said before, our livelihood depends upon it.'

Jack cautiously nods. John Wayne then taps the driver on his shoulder and says, 'Drive.'

Later That Evening

Chapter Forty-Seven

Redy has been lying on the cold concrete for almost eight hours as forensic officers search for evidence. He lies behind a white screen. In front of the screen are huddles of people; a few women are crying, others are offering comforting hugs. On cars and on walls sit the man-dem, some holding back tears for the loss of a person they would describe as being the safest guy who didn't deserve to die this way.

Redy's big brother, Vino, who is sitting on Paro's car, says to Thomas, 'He didn't deserve to go out like this.' He shakes his head. 'Nah, bruv, he didn't deserve this.' Vino lowers his head as he chokes back tears.

Thomas puts his hand on Vino's shoulder and pictures Redy walking out of his bedroom saying that he'll be back in awhile, not knowing that moment was going to be the last time he would ever see Redy walking and breathing.

Thomas closes his eyes and squeezes Vino's shoulder. 'Mi know, cuz, mi know... Redy was ah good yute.' Thomas sucks his teeth. 'Redy never deserve dis.'

From out the blackness of the night, two beams of lights come shooting towards where Thomas, Vino and Paro dwell. The guys all look towards the light, which belongs to a car, which is now carrying John Wayne and Jack, but no-one else. John Wayne and Jack jump out of the car.

'All right, fellas?' says John Wayne as he steps up to the man-dem. No-one answers him verbally; they only respond with faint chin nods.

'I am Detective Chief Inspector Wain—' John Wayne motions towards Jack '—and this is my colleague Detective Constable Mills. We're from a Special Unit in Trident. Did you see anything or do you know anything or did you know the victim?'

With a cold expression, Vino says, 'Yeah, I knew him, he was my little brother.'

'OK—' John Wayne takes out a pad and pen. 'Can you tell me a bit about his background?'

Without his expression changing, Vino says, 'Why are you here? Why do you exist?'

'I am here to try and catch these bastards that killed your brother. I exist to try and get rid of black on black gun crime from our streets.'

Vino sniggers, which lets out a high pitch laugh, then says, 'It's a pity you didn't try and get rid of black on black gun crime when it first started back in the day… Do you know how much people have died from guns on the streets of Brixton and all over London? And for years no one didn't do anything.' Vino gets up from the car. 'Listen, I don't know what your agenda is…but your so called help is a little too late… it's not guns you have to get off the streets.' Vino pokes his finger in the side of his head. 'It's this ignorant mentality.' Vino sucks his teeth and walks over to his crying mum who has just turned up with Redy's girlfriend and two children.

Chapter Forty-Eight

John Wayne doesn't bother asking Thomas or Paro any further questions. Him and Jack get back into their car and drive off leaving Paro and Thomas to get into Paro's car.

Moments later Peon, who went to school with Redy, walks over to Paro's car with Vino behind him. The men get in the car. Peon stares out of the window. The corners of his mouth turn down towards his chin. Peon is pissed, double pissed that no revenge was taken on the people who robbed him and now they have killed his old school friend. Peon wants revenge. He demands revenge.

Thomas turns to Peon. 'My lawd, yuh sure?'

Peon replies with a tear in his eye and a lump of sorrow in his throat, 'Of course I'm sure, it was dat pussy hole Gunn and his idiat Muslim Brudders, init.'

Vino turns to Peon. 'Who told you this?'

Peon's right eye twitches. 'Some man-dem from da bits, init. Bruv, look are we gonna do something bout dis or wot?'

Paro clears his throat. 'Rudeboy, listen, it's not dat

easy, rudeboy d'you get me? You think we can just roll up in Baghdad just like dat, rudeboy?'

Peon looks towards the distance where the housing blocks of Myatts Fields North stand. He shrugs. 'Why not? So dey can just rob me and kill Redy just like dat?'

Silence falls inside the car. It is then broken by Vino. 'Can you get guns?'

Peon's eyes widen slightly which indicates his shock at Vino's ignorant question. 'Hey, Vino, tings dun change, you know… I know you've been out of town for long but Brixton is now called Bang-Bang Bricky, bruv.'

Peon pulls back snot into the back of his throat and states, 'Course I can get guns, a ten year old boy can get a gun.'

Vino had moved into a quiet part of South London where the ghetto of Brixton seemed a whole world apart. He had moved there with his wife of two years. Vino had grown up on Stockwell Park Housing Estate so he is no stranger to beef but had worked hard to get away from those situations. Vino put himself through college then university and got himself a good job but now seems to be willing to throw that all away. Vino looks at Peon with a steely look that makes his eyebrows wrinkle up and says, 'Well done the talk then init, just get them and we will deal with the case.'

Everyone stares out of the car window at the white screen that's hiding Redy's decomposing body.

A Week Later

Chapter Forty-Nine

Myatts Fields has no one walking through it as the time hits 10:45 P.M. Redy's body had been picked up from behind the white screen five days before. He had lain there for almost two days, without any conclusive forensic evidence being found.

Fifteen minutes ago, on a block landing in Myatts Fields—Barmah Green, Crawshay Court, which is a stones throw away from where Redy's body had fallen—stood Gunn and a few of his Muslim brothers. They had heard three days ago that possibly revenge would be taken on behalf of Redy. They're not worried as they leave the block to take care of some business.

Moments later, four young males and two young females from a new gang called O Tray, roll up on the block and congregate where Gunn and his Muslim brothers were standing. The O Tray gang, like the PIF gang (Paid In Full) and the OC gang (Organize Crime) are all a branch off from the PDC crew. The PIF gang wear Purple; the OC gang wear Green; and the O Tray gang wear Red like their infamous American counterparts the Bloods gang.

Two of the males are in an argument. 'Nah, gee,' says one of the yutes to the other, 'dis Muslim ting is taking over da streets, gee. Dese akhis are on dis ting. Dey're peeling everyone and anyone who's not Muslim. I've even heard ber mans getting licked down if you're not turning Muslim, blud.'

'U'listing bun dat,' the other replies. 'I'm rolling wid da cross, u'listing.' The yute sucks his teeth. 'I don't care dem Muslim brudders can't do me nuttin', u'listing. I'm from Brixton, so I'm a bad man. Yeah, I'm big man, u'listing.'

A voice shoots down the landing. 'Oi, Pesky, shut your mouth,' says the voice, which comes from a boy named Malo who is a few years older than the congregation of yutes.

Pesky and the rest of the yutes turn around. Malo curls his lips and repeats himself, 'Yeah, shut up you dickhead, on da bits chatting shit. Stop chatting shit and you're not a big man.'

Pesky pushes out his chest. 'Wot, I am a big man.'

'How are you a big man?'

Pesky raises his eyebrows. 'U'listing, because I've got a big dick, init, and when I wuk ber big woman I mek dem scream, u'listing.'

All the yutes laugh. A smile forms on Malo's usually serious face. The two young females say, 'Wot, show us your dick den.'

Pesky is about to pull out his penis when both of the females scream as a symphony of gunshots whiz down the landing.

Chapter Fifty

The bullets that come flying down the landing hit both the girls and miss all the guys, including Malo.

Malo is packing. He runs as he returns fire at the shooters: Thomas, Paro and Peon. Vino has been left behind; well, forced behind by his wife when she found out what he was going to do.

Malo's chest is burning as he reaches Fairbairn Green, Treherne Court, a block that is opposite Barmah Green, Crawshay Court. He runs up the brick slope past the smelly bin chutes and towards the first house on the left. Malo knocks the door; moments later it opens.

Najash looks down at Malo. 'Wot's going on akhi?'

Malo breathes heavy through his nose. 'Some yutes just rolled up on da block and started bussing.'

Najash opens up the door wide. 'Wot?! True stories? Where?'

Malo points his thumb over his shoulder. 'Over dere, on Crawshay Court.'

Najash runs back into the house. He comes back out with four other Muslim brothers; they're all strapped.

They make their way with speed over to Crawshay Court.

Malo sits down on the wall outside the house to catch his breath. Moments later he's joined by a guy called Abdual-Hakim who is one of Gunn's right hand men. Abdual-Hakim grew up on the middle class side of Brixton Hill. He attended the same school as Gunn after being transferred from his private school by his white middle class parents who wanted to prove that public school could provide as good an education as a private school.

'Assalamu alaikum,' says Abdual-Hakim as he brushes down his blonde beard. Although Abdual-Hakim is white he speaks like, and even resembles, his black Muslim brothers regarding their mannerisms and dress sense. He also has something else in common with his black brothers: Abdual-Hakim is related to Gunn, Paro and Thomas through him being a direct descendant from an African slave who was the brother of these guys' great, great, great, great grandfather.

You can tell by the pupils of Malo's eyes he is still in shock. 'Wa alaikums salam,' replies Malo finally.

Abdual-Hakim rolls his phone in his hand. 'So wot, was dese yutes masked up?'

'Yeah, ak,' says Malo in an even tone. 'But, I heard one of dem call the other's name.'

With eagerness in his eyes, Abdual-Hakim says, 'Naam, wot was da name?'

'Paro—I'm sure I heard one of dem say Paro.'

Abdual-Hakim bites his top lip. 'Paro? Ter.' He dials for Gunn. 'Assalamu alaikum.'

'Wa alaikums salam wa rahmatullah,' replies Gunn.

'Hey, akhi, you never gonna guess wot…? Paro and some next yutes rolled up in Baghdad letting off shots, ahki. Real talks.'

The line goes silent for a second, then Gunn says, 'Say no more… give me an hour, salam.'

Chapter Fifty-One

Gunn walks out of his mother's front door wearing a long coat and hat. His conscience is riding him. He rubs his chin and says to himself, 'Bruv, you've gotta get yourself out of dis gang ting. Dis ain't part of Islam.' With steady footsteps, Gunn walks over to a waiting car. He jumps in. The car takes off, and seconds later an unmarked police car pulls out of a parking space and follows.

'Shit, it's da Jakes.'

'Wot, Da Boy-Dem?' says Gunn.

'Yeah, it's Da Boy-Dem, dey're behind us,' replies Driver.

Gunn looks into the side mirror and picks up the police car and the face of Jack, the fresh-face officer. John Wayne has sent Jack on this surveillance while he remains at the station in communication via radio and a video link that is recording the trailing of Gunn's car.

'OK, Jack,' says John Wayne, 'just stay close. They know you are on to them, so there is no need to keep discreet.'

'OK, Sir, but I still fail to see the point of this exercise. We should cease the opportunity and nick them now.'

'All in good time, Jack.'

'OK, Sir.' Jack points to the left and says to the driver, 'They've turned left.'

The driver moves over two lanes and swerves into the road that Gunn's car has turned into. Gunn's car shoots up a narrow street that leads to Norwood Road —a road that leads to Brixton.

Gunn turns to Driver. 'Slow down, bruv.'

Driver slows down the car. He reaches out onto Norwood Road and travels down it at a steady pace. Jack is still up behind.

Driver reaches outside the back of Brockwell Park. He heads up towards two main sets of traffic lights that split the traffic off to either Camberwell or Brixton. Driver dwells over which way he should take to get to Myatts Fields. He reaches the set of traffic lights and both are green. Driver swerves the car out to the far right and heads for Camberwell. He looks in his rearview mirror and sees the police car bearing to the left for Brixton.

'Yes!' says Driver. 'Da devil dem 'r gone.'

With composure Gunn says, 'Naam, fire bun da Jakes. Come let's go and get Abdullah den blow to Baghdad.'

Chapter Fifty-Two

"B aghdad" is set alight with argument because one of the girls who got shot is Najash's sister.

'Oi, Najash, calm down, bruv,' says Abdual-Hakim. 'Gunn soon reach.'

Najash's face contorts with rage as his voice booms down the landing like thunder. 'HOW YOU MEAN, CALM DOWN? ARE YOU STUPID?' Najash punches the air with his long but muscular arm. 'My little sister just got a bullet through her leg and you're telling me to calm down.'

Abdual-Hakim swallows hard. 'Akhi, I know, akhi, but we have to wait for Gunn, akhi.'

'Fire bun, Gunn.' Najash slams his bony fist into his palm. 'And I don't even know why we're following someone who is due to be an informer. Look how much case he's bust.' Najash pauses, realizing he has let out his true feelings about Gunn. He looks at everyone to see who might snitch, then thinks he couldn't care less. He calmly continues. 'We don't need Gunn, yeah. We know where da yute lives so let's roll up dere now.' Najash looks across to the other Muslim brothers—no-one makes a comment. Najash looks at Malo. 'Oi, akhi, come here.'

Malo walks over and nods. 'Yeah?'

'Oi, you said Paro was one of da shotters, yeah?'

'Yeah, I didn't see his face but I heard one of da others call his name, init.'

Najash turns to Abdual-Hakim. 'You see, so wot we waiting for? Let's do dis ting. I know where Paro lives. Let's roll up to his yard now, init.'

Abdual-Hakim is filled with stress. He grits his teeth and his palms become sweaty. 'Najash, I know, bruv, but still yet, we have to wait for Gunn.'

A large vein pops out of Najash's neck. 'I said fire bun, Gunn. Look how long he's taking to come. Nah, I don't even care, I'm rolling up dere by myself den, init.' Najash shouts to his girlfriend. 'Oi, Denise, go and get my gun.'

Abdual-Hakim scratches his head. He looks at the time on his phone then at the others. 'So wot, are you lot on dis ting?'

Everyone nods. 'A'ight, let's roll out den.'

Najash, Abdual-Hakim and the rest of Gunn's Muslim brothers roll out to Paro's mum's house.

Chapter Fifty-Three

Abdullah takes twenty minutes to get out of his wifey's house. He has just been released from prison after doing eight out of a ten-year sentence. He is now in the car, which still smells of chicken and leather, with Gunn and Driver looking relaxed in the front seats.

'So wot, you really telling me, akhi, Paro and some next yutes rolled up in Baghdad bussing off shots?' Abdullah shakes his head. 'Are you serious?'

'Yeah, ak, real talks,' responds Driver.

Abdullah sucks on his teeth and addresses Gunn. 'So wot, ak, who were dese other yutes wid him?'

Gunn cracks his knuckles. 'Boy, I don't even know,' Gunn replies in a dry tone of voice, 'but I feel say it must be Peon, init, and even Redy's big brother, Vino.'

Driver shakes his head. 'Nah, ak, didn't I tell you? Some chick just text me about half hour ago and said it was Paro, Peon and Redy's cousin, some yute from yard called Tommy Terrible.'

Gunn's eyes turn stone cold at the thought of a "Yardie" coming into Baghdad and bussing shots;

especially shots that where meant for him. 'Wot? You didn't tell me dis.'

Driver pulls the car into Mostyn Road that leads up to Myatts Fields. 'Rah, I thought I told you, ak?'

Gunn sucks on his teeth. 'Bruv, you smoke too much weed, you know. You need to get on your deen and stop smoking weed, akhi.'

Driver steers the car over to the entrance of Myatts Fields. 'Just cool, man.'

A blacked out space cruiser speeds out of the estate.

'Rah, who's dat? Da Boy-Dem?' asks Abdullah.

'Yeah, due to be,' says Gunn as he pushes back into the chair. 'Da idiats were following us before we come to pick you up.'

Abdullah looks out of the window. 'Cha, it's bout time we pepper deir skin, you know.'

Gunn nods. 'Don't worry, their time will come, mashallah.' He calls Abdual-Hakim's phone as Driver drives up to Barmah Green.

Chapter Fifty-Four

Najash, Abdual-Hakim and the rest of Gunn's Muslim brothers pull onto Landor Road, a road that connects Stockwell, Brixton and Clapham. Abdual-Hakim's phone rings; it's Gunn. He contemplates answering, looks at Najash whose eyes are focused ahead on his mission, and rejects the call. Then turns off the phone. 'Yeah, it's dis left here, you know,' he says to Najash.

Najash turns the car into Dalyell Road, the Brixton side of Landor Road. 'Oi, he lives at number one hundred and eighteen, init?

'Yeah, I think so,' replies Abdual-Hakim.

Najash continues up Dalyell Road, slowing down for the road humps. Abdual-Hakim's heart pounds as Najash pulls over to the left. One hundred and eighteen comes into view opposite.

Abdual-Hakim talks slowly. 'OK, listen, yeah—' He looks at Najash '—just knock, yeah, and when da door answers don't rush up in dere—'

Najash cuts in. 'Yeah, yeah, whatever.' He finishes loading his gun and gets out of the car followed by one of the Muslim brothers who was sitting in the back with another.

'Oi, ak, bring him back to da car.' Abdual-Hakim's words fall on deaf ears.

Najash is in a different zone...the "killing zone". He reaches the door and knocks it hard...

Then harder still...

No answer.

Najash steps back from the door, and looks up at the windows and sees movement. He knocks the door again and rings the bell. He hears movement. He waits awhile then knocks and rings again. Pissed off, Najash walks back to the car. 'Damn,' he says as he opens the car door. 'Someone is in and dey won't answer da door.'

Abdual-Hakim looks up at Najash. 'Well, bruv, let's go. We'll catch him on da rebound.'

Najash's eyebrows close together. 'Cha, I don't even wanna go because I swear he's in dere.' Najash recalls the crying from his sister, which releases an uncontrollable rage that consumes him. 'Nah, I'm pissed.' Najash sucks his teeth. 'Naam, if he doesn't wanna come out I'm gonna make him come out.' Najash pulls out his gun.

'Oi, ak, wot you doing?' shouts Abdual-Hakim as he pops open the car door.

Before Abdual-Hakim can get out of the car, a ricochet of bullets from Najash's gun blast through the windows of Paro's mum's house.

The Following Day

Chapter Fifty-Five

The talk in Brixton is about the shooting up of Paro's mum's house. The talk on road by some other people is that Gunn did the shooting.

Outside, on Fiveways Road in Angell Town, the largest single development project in Brixton, which was named after a family that owned land in Lambeth and where a grimy block landing once stood, stand some yutes from the PIF, OC and O Tray gang who are discussing the shooting. One of the yutes is Pesky; the same yute that claimed he's a big man because he has a big penis.

Pesky leans on a wall of a house that has sweet smelling stew chicken emitting from it. He kisses his teeth. 'Yeah, u'listing, I heard dat Gunn sprayed up da yard, init.'

A youth from the OC gang says, 'For real, don't lie?'

Pesky wipes his mouth. 'Yeah, I heard dat Gunn buss ber shots through Paro's mum's window, u'listing. And den he ran up in da yard and started shanking everyone, u'listing.' Pesky shakes his head. 'Liberties, I know, Gunn's a bad boy but he should of never have done dat, u'listing.'

A member of the O Tray gang says, 'Why not? It come in like you don't remember dat just da other day Paro was bussing shots after us.'

Pesky bites the inside of his mouth. 'Yeah, I know, but he wasn't bussing after us, u'listing, he wasn't after us.'

'So wot? A bullet don't have no name, you know,' states the now-angry O Tray gang member, whose nostrils are flaring.

Feeling like an ignoramus, Pesky says, 'Anyway, I heard dere's gonna be mad beef on road now, u'listing, cos Paro's uncle is one bad man named Natty-Nya. An old time bad man, u'listing, I heard nuff people has tried to kill his uncle ber times, u'listing, but his uncle can't dead.' Pesky looks at everyone to see if he has their full attention, then continues the legend of Natty-Nya. 'U'listing, every time his uncle kills someone he has to go to Africa and eat a human heart, so he doesn't get killed, u'listing.'

Some of the group suck their teeth, and a member of the PIF gang shouts, 'Bun dat, dat's some science ting, man don't work ina science. Astaghfirullah.'

Pesky coughs a nervous laugh, whilst the PIF gang member and two other OC members, who have had enough of listening to Pesky, depart.

Pesky continues with his tales about Natty-Nya, who in actuality had left the bad man business years ago and now has a degree in biological immortality, and therefore will not be taking any revenge upon Gunn.

A Few Hours Later

Chapter Fifty-Six

John Wayne, his boys, and a news film crew are inside Paro's mum's house, one hundred and eighteen Dalyell Road.

Paro's mum slowly comes down the stairs bringing her usual sprayed on scent of green marine and fruit with her as she meets her guests.

John Wayne extends his hand. 'Good afternoon. Are you Ms. Nicholas?'

Ms. Nicholas's eyes are red like cherries from all the crying she's been doing. She nods wearily.

'Hi. I am Detective Chief Inspector Wain and this is my colleague Detective Constable Mills.' John Wayne looks over at Jack. 'We are from a Special Unit in Trident. We are also here with a news crew to get an exclusive interview regarding this terrible incident on your home.'

Ms. Nicholas again nods. 'OK.'

She leads her guests into her dining room. The windows are boarded up. Ms. Nicholas sits on one of her dining table chairs.

John Wayne and the news crew are standing up. The

reporter leading the interview shakes Ms. Nicholas's hand and says, 'Hi, Ms. Nicholas, I am Sarah Jones, I will be conducting the interview. I will just be asking you why you think guns and violence have gone so out of control recently and what can be done to curb it.'

Ms. Nicholas raises her eyebrows and calmly says, 'Guns and violence is nothing new to Brixton; it's existed for donkey years.' Ms. Nicholas looks across at everyone standing in front of her. 'You know, I've seen a lot happen down here in Brixton in the 70s, 80s and 90s. During that time the media seemed not to be interested in the shootings, stabbings, beheadings—yes, beheadings; some poor soul had their head chopped off up there on Coldharbour Lane back in the eighties.' Ms. Nicholas folds her arms. 'That didn't make the news, but I can guess why it didn't.' Ms. Nicholas wipes the corners of her eyes. 'Look, I just think all this palava is just a little too late. These kids are out of control and it's gonna take more than news interviews and campaigns against guns to control them.' Ms. Nicholas covers her face with her open palms. Tears spring out of her eyes and roll down her face.

The room falls silent for a moment.

'OK. Everyone lets leave Ms. Nicholas for awhile,' says John Wayne, breaking the silence and herding everyone out of Ms. Nicholas's house.

Chapter Fifty-Seven

The news crew is hulled around their van while Jack, John Wayne and his men are outside their silver blacked-out space cruiser. They are drinking tea and arguing.

'Sir, why can we not just pick up these scumbags right now and get them off the streets?'

John Wayne, in a diplomatic voice, says, 'I know it is hard to see the aftermath and deal with the anguish coming from innocent third parties but we as professionals have to remain professional.' John Wayne takes a sip of his tea. 'Look, I know it seems the tactics I am employing seem highly unethical, but trust me, under the surface this is how the system has always operated. The system is in business to cause or create problems because as long as there are problems that need solving, the system will always be needed.' John Wayne laughs. 'Do you think it is a coincidence that all the violence and death that happened in Brixton over the years hardly ever made the news?' John Wayne's men make no comment. John Wayne shakes his head. 'It was all part of a divine plan, everything from the conception of bringing over a massive group of ignorant Jamaicans back in the forties and trapping them in England's first black ghetto.'

John Wayne takes another sip of his tea. 'The powers that be were relying on these long term problems to arise. They set it in motion and spun a web for these bastards.' John Wayne looks at all his men with stern eyes. 'When I get the word to pick up these slags that is when we will move and not a minute sooner.'

A call comes through on John Wayne's phone; he takes it while walking away from his men and throwing away his cup of tea.

Chapter Fifty-Eight

Back over in Myatts Fields—"Baghdad"—the block is once again in an eruption of argument.

Gunn is doing his best not to bring bodily harm to Najash. 'You're just a tall lanky doughnut, you know. First you burst Redy, like a mad-man. Why, I don't know why? Den you blaze up Paro's mum's yard, almost killing his two little sisters.' Gunn taps his finger on his temple. 'Are you stupid, akhi? Taqhelaire, akhi. Haraam. Jahill!'

Najash looks to the floor and rubs his shaped-up bushy beard, then kisses his teeth. 'Naam,' he says looking back up. 'Listen, yeah, I wasn't myself dat night.' Najash holds up his hands. 'A'ight , fair enough, I went sick, init. I shouldn't have done it, but astaghfirullah...my yute could have killed my little sister.' Najash runs his tongue over his lips. 'Eye for an eye, astaghfirullah.'

Gunn squints his right eye. 'So is dat how you look at it, yeah?'

'Sure bloody, and plus Paro's a kuffar. OK, he's an old school dude but he's still a kuffar. He's an infidel.

Faithless. Dem man dere must get found in da bushes faceless.' Najash laughs. 'You get me doe?' He moves to each of the Muslim brothers tapping their fist with his. 'Alhamdulillah, man.'

Gunn jerks his head up and down. 'Say no more, akhi, Alhamdulillah.' His eyes roll dead serious. 'Dis is not a warning but don't ever do a move again widout hollering at me first.'

Najash squints. He embraces Gunn. 'Inshallah, ak.'

Gunn's phone rings. He releases from Najash's embrace and answers. 'Talk. Wot...? Are you sure...?' Gunn looks at Najash, and then continues talking to the person on the other end of the phone. 'A'ight, say no more. Hold him dere until I come.' Gunn ends the call and says to everyone, 'Come, let's roll.'

All the Muslim brothers roll out to ambush Peon who is in the company of a sexy female.

Chapter Fifty-Nine

Gunn and his Muslim brothers, who are all strapped, pull out of Myatts Fields in a black coupe. Trailing behind is John Wayne and his boys.

'OK, Phil, keep a nice easy distance,' John Wayne instructs the driver.

Jack clears his throat. 'I am going to be honest, Sir. I do not think I can stand to see these wankers do any more criminal activities and turn a blind eye.'

John Wayne looks at Jack. 'Jack, the time is coming soon. I will be getting the word very soon.'

'I know, Sir, I know. I just wish you could get the word now. I so badly want these scum of the slums off the streets.' Jack nods and smiles. 'Yeah, that will really start to make me sleep easy at night.'

John Wayne looks ahead and smirks. 'Jack, I have got bad news for you, for as long as you stay in this business you will never sleep easy at night.' John Wayne's eyes light up. 'Because for every one of them—' John Wayne motions at the car that Gunn and his Muslim brothers are in '—that we nick and put behind bars, another one takes their place.' John

Wayne looks over at Jack. 'And let me tell you one of the reasons why there is always someone to fill that place.' John Wayne looks forward and flicks the tip of his long nose. 'Because the majority of these black bastards are ignorant.' John Wayne pauses then continues: 'The cause... because they refuse to read books.' John Wayne laughs to himself. 'That is why I call them animals because only animals do not read books.' John Wayne coughs suddenly. 'And what is the result...? Killing each other; generation after generation for money and respect.'

Jack raises his eyebrows and looks out of the window. He says to himself, 'What have I got myself into?'

John Wayne breaks his thoughts. 'Listen, I made my career out of this "black on black" killing cycle and you can too, but you must have an open mind to deal with the ugly reality of our job.' In a warm tone, John Wayne reassures. 'Jack, do not worry too much because there is this Jamaican proverb that goes: time is longer than rope, which means time will hang these niggers soon enough.'

John Wayne's car turns off Acre Lane and follows Gunn's car down towards Sandmere Road, a road that connects Brixton to Clapham.

Chapter Sixty

Driver is almost at the end of Ballater Road, which connects to Sandmere Road. He looks in his rearview mirror and spots John Wayne trailing him. He turns to Gunn. 'Oh shit, Da Boy-Dem is behind us again.'

Gunn looks in the side mirror. Driver turns left into Sandmere Road. Gunn instructs; 'A'ight, ak, just keep on driving.'

Driver continues down Sandmere Road: John Wayne's car follows up behind. Gunn, Driver, and the two other Muslim brothers who are in the back, all look to the left as the house that Peon is being seduced in comes into view. Gunn sucks his teeth. Driver looks at him. 'So wot are we gonna do, ak? Drive out da Jakes and come back later?'

Gunn shakes his head. 'Nah, dat's not gonna work, my girl can't hold Peon all day. She told me dat he's been dere since last night and he's looking to blow in a hot minute.' Gunn looks in his side view mirror again, then says, 'Dutty Boy-Dem. Shaitan.'

Driver brakes the car as he comes to the end of

Sandmere Road. John Wayne's car stops two cars away. Driver pulls out to the right onto Bedford Road, which leads to Landor Road that will take him back to Myatts Fields.

Gunn's phone rings with an unknown number. He doesn't answer it. Moments later the phone rings back with a number. He answers it. 'Talk.'

'Hi, babes, it's Leandra.'

'Who?'

'Leandra,' she says, feeling like dirt on realizing that Gunn doesn't remember her.

Gunn thinks: oh, dat one pop wid da messy yard. Cha, wot does she want? Gunn coughs. 'Oh, wot's going on?'

Leandra licks her big lips. 'I've got some information for you.' Leandra looks at the dirty plates that lay on her table. 'It's about your girlfriend...someone told me she's banging one Yardie from da ends.' Gunn remains silent and Leandra continues: 'If you wanna find out who she's banging be at my house tonight.'

Leandra hangs up the phone. Gunn kisses his teeth and looks into the side mirror at John Wayne's car still following him as Driver heads towards Myatts Fields.

Chapter Sixty-One

Inside Leandra's messy house she gets up as her intercom bell rings; it's Thomas. He had strolled into Myatts Fields South to waylay Gunn inside Leandra's house. He had known Leandra from Jamaica and met her up again opposite Brockwell Park in a wine bar that used to be called Brockwells.

Leandra opens her door and speaks in her Jamaican accent. 'Waah gwaan, mi dupes?'

Thomas steps into the house and is hit with the stench of cigarettes and a dirty kitchen. 'Cool nah, man,' says Thomas as he kisses Leandra's lips and squeezes her round solid big bum.

Leandra leads Thomas into her sitting room. Thomas steps towards the curtain and looks out of the window. 'Yuh set it up?'

'Yeah, man. Mi feel seh him a cum.' Leandra sits down.

Thomas glares at her. 'Yuh sure?'

Leandra replies with a reassuring nod.

'Cho,' Thomas narrows his eyes, 'im fi dead yuh nuh, yuh si it.'

'Yeah, man a true, im fi dead yes.'

Thomas shakes his head with conviction. 'Jah know, a how im fi kill mi cousin, an a did wan good yute. Mi a tell yuh, man. It ah guh sweet mi when mi kill im. Caah si when im dead Brixtan a fi mi, yuh si it?' Thomas pokes his finger in his chest then walks away from the window. 'Yeah, man. Brixtan a fi mi an dis sheggrie Muslim ting dunn, mi a tell yuh, babes.'

Leandra smiles. Thomas picks her up and runs his hands down her bottom. 'Weh di gun deh?'

'Inna di bedroom.'

Thomas laughs. 'Come mek wi guh in deh an wait pan dis bwoy yah.'

Leandra leads Thomas into her bedroom but not just to wait on Gunn to arrive but also to wait until Thomas ejaculates inside of her.

Chapter Sixty-Two

The time is eleven o'clock at night. Leandra has given Thomas three rounds of hardcore sex, but this still hasn't made up for Gunn not arriving at her house.

Thomas kicks his legs out of the bed. 'Call di bwoy aggen nuh.'

Leandra eases herself up in the bed. 'Im nah ansa im phone.'

Thomas looks around at her. 'How yuh mean im naah ansa im phone. Jus awhile agguh yuh sey it switch haf.'

Leandra wrinkles her forehead and talks in her British accent. 'Yeah I mean his phone is turned off, init.'

Thomas kisses his teeth and gets off the bed. 'Cho, yuh a idiat gal, man. Mek mi deh roun yuh yawd fi hours an di bwoy nuh cum.' He rubs his head. 'Cho, a weh mi pants dem deh?'

His jeans are over in the corner next to three dirty drinking glasses. He walks over to them and puts them on while saying, 'Suh a whey yuh tell di yute when yuh call im?'

Leandra bites her lip and switches back to patois. 'Mi jus tell im seh smaddy tell mi seh im gal dida screw pan im an if im waah fi fine out a who shi dida bang den im fi come a mi house tinite.'

Thomas kisses his teeth again. 'Bloodclaat a weh duh dis idiat gal?' Thomas grits his pearly white teeth. 'A how yuh fi tell...?' Thomas shakes his head and says, 'Cho, bumboclaat,' then walks towards the door.

Leandra jumps out of the bed and flips back to British. 'But he still might come, for him dis is still early.'

Thomas opens the door. 'Im naah cum, man. Listen falla mi go outta road.'

Chapter Sixty-Three

Out on Brixton Road Gunn is driving his wifey's car. She's sitting beside him. The couple are coming from watching a late night movie.

Gunn slows down to a stop at the traffic lights. Without looking at his wifey, Gunn says, 'Someone told me sutum today.' Gunn grips the steering wheel and laughs. 'Someone told me dat you're giving me bun.'

Gunn's wifey stays quiet. The traffic lights change.

'Cadija, did you just hear wot I said?'

Cadija looks at Gunn. 'Ah come on, babes, you of all people shouldn't be listening to gossip. That's just bad mind talk. You know what the roads are like.'

Cadija looks away from Gunn with a glint of nervousness in her eyes as she remembers the moment she gave Thomas her phone number inside Satay Bar.

Gunn flares his nostrils. 'Hmm.' He drives through the traffic lights and continues down Brixton Road.

Cadija goes into her purse, takes out her lip-gloss and applies it; she always does this when she is nervous. 'Anyway, how do I know what you're up to when you disappear for over a week?' Cadija rubs her lips together.

'Forget bout dat,' Gunn says, 'we're not talking bout dat. We're talking bout you giving me bun, ter. Listen, you know wot I'll do to you if I ever find out dat you're giving me bun.'

A chill runs down Cadija's spine. She doesn't answer; this is sufficient enough to make Gunn know she understands the repercussions from his warning.

Gunn slows down the car again, but this time to pull into a petrol station. Gunn stops at a petrol pump and jumps out of the car.

Opposite the petrol station are rows of shops, selling everything from Fish & Chips to Chinese food. There is a sweetie shop, which is closed, and an Off-Licence, which is about to close at eleven thirty. The time is now eleven twenty-five.

Gunn looks across the road at the Off-Licence. He sees Leandra paying for her alcohol. Gunn opens the car door. 'Wait here, I'll be back in a minute.' He slams it shut and makes his way over to Leandra.

Chapter Sixty-Four

Leandra takes her change from the Asian shop-keeper and steps out of the shop.

'Oi!'

Leandra stops and looks to her right. Her heart feels like it has jump into her mouth as she sees Gunn storming over to her. Leandra looks up towards the Chinese takeaway, which Thomas is inside. She hopes that he'll come out and save her from what Gunn may do to her.

'Oi!'

Leandra looks away from the Chinese takeaway. Gunn is now in her face.

'Oi, don't you hear me calling you?'

Leandra swallows hard. 'Oh, you a'ight, babes?'

Gunn sucks his teeth and squints. 'Oi, you're rass-clart taking liberties, you know.' Gunn pokes Leandra in the side of her head.

Leandra shouts loud in her Jamaican accent, 'A WEY YUH A DUH?!'

Gunn raises his fist as if to thump Leandra in her

mouth as Thomas walks out of the Chinese takeaway. Thomas steps slightly back into the shop as Gunn pulls his fist away from Leandra's face. Slowly, she recoils from her flinch.

Thomas bites on his bottom lip and wishes he had brought the gun out with him. 'Cha, mi could end dis bwoy now,' he says to himself.

Thomas hits his fist into his left palm, and then cracks his knuckles. He taps his back pocket and feels his flick knife. His eyes flip into what look like the eyes of an animal that is about to brutally kill its prey.

Thomas flicks out his knife and approaches Gunn.

Chapter Sixty-Five

Thomas is now a few feet behind Gunn. He has his knife ready to do some damage.

Gunn snarls at Leandra. 'Mine I knock out your teeth, you know.'

Gunn is about to add that if Leandra doesn't keep his girlfriend's name out of her mouth he will definitely kick out all of her teeth when a sharp pain penetrates his back.

'Arhhhhh.' Gunn falls forward. His wifey screams from inside the car. Before Gunn can turn around, Thomas stabs him in his back again. Leandra takes her bottle of alcohol out of her bag.

Gunn turns around and with quick lightning reflex, blocks the bottle that Leandra throws at him. The bottle smashes over his arm. Blood bursts out of Gunn's elbow as Thomas rushes into him with the knife.

'Kill him!' screams Leandra.

Thomas plunges the tip of his knife into Gunn's side; it won't go any further. Gunn is holding Thomas's wrist with all his strength.

Cadija is now crying, but dares not to come out of

the car and help her boyfriend.

Gunn headbutts Thomas…then again. Thomas falls back releasing the tip of the blade out of Gunn.

Leandra screams again. 'Kill di bwoy, man.' She runs towards Gunn with a brick aiming for his head. Before she can launch the brick, a red car screeches to a halt. Malo jumps out. He kicks Leandra in her side. She drops the brick and flies towards the floor. Malo grips Thomas around the neck and swings him away from Gunn.

Cadija stops crying and terminates the call she was going to make to the police as she watches if the beef is still going to continue.

Chapter Sixty-Six

Blood drips out of Gunn's side and down his leg. He stares at his attackers who are picking themselves up from the floor.

Malo runs to his car and pulls out a baseball bat. Thomas clenches his knife as fear enters his eyes.

Malo swings the bat in the air. 'Listen, I'm gonna mash you up, you little Yardies.'

Thomas doesn't reply. Leandra runs behind him. Malo heads to the pair, planning to do the most damage a baseball bat can do.

Gunn grabs after him. 'Nah, akhi, laowit.'

'Wot, are you sure, ak?'

'Yeah, man, just cool,' replies Gunn.

Malo points the bat at Thomas and Leandra. 'Nah, dey must get deir heads bust, man.'

Gunn grips Malo's arm and pulls him towards his car. 'I said cool, put back da bat.'

Malo hesitates for a second as the late night traffic slows down to take a look at the commotion. Malo sucks on his teeth and walks back to his car.

Fear leaves Thomas's eyes. Gunn makes direct eye

contact with him. He stares him out for a moment or two, then points and says, 'Remember I told you, yeah, da next time you see me, you better have your gun on you.'

Thomas doesn't reply as his heart pounds in his chest. Gunn glances at Leandra then smoothly steps away from the spot he could have died in.

The Following Morning

Chapter Sixty-Seven

Hours after the attack on Gunn, word had got back to John Wayne from his best informant. Him and his boys are now outside Gunn's rented flat which is in Tulse Hill, an area in Brixton named after the Tulse family who owned the area back in the 1650s when Brixton was mostly farmland.

Gunn steps out of his flat with his manbag strapped over his shoulder… snap, goes the sound of the police camera. Gunn opens the door to the black hatch back… snap. He gets in… snap. The car drives off… snap.

'That's the same bag he had last time, Chief,' says the officer with the large head as he removes the camera from his eye.

John Wayne nods. 'Yeah, OK. Ray, follow them.'

Ray the driver pulls out and trails Gunn's car.

Looking straight ahead, John Wayne says to his boys, 'Lads, I have good news. We are taking him down tomorrow.'

Jack clears his throat from the back seat. 'At last, thank God for that. So what are we bringing him down on?'

John Wayne smiles. 'Well, hopefully his reaction from the altercation he had last night. My informant tells me the person is as good as dead.'

Jack shakes his head. 'So what happens if he does not kill this person? What then?'

John Wayne's right eye twitches. 'Not to worry about that, Jack. That person will be killed and Mr. Boor will be our man.' John Wayne covers his mouth as he coughs. 'Besides, when do we ever need evidence to bring a black bastard to court and have him put on remand for a year to two years? All we need is good grounds and sometimes if the grounds are good enough we could even get a conviction. I think I have created very good grounds if this person is not killed.'

Gunn's car is now on Norwood Road; it bears to the right as it approaches the traffic lights that split the traffic off to Brixton or Camberwell. His car takes the route to Camberwell heading for Kings College Hospital, a place he was born back in 1983.

Later That Day

Chapter Sixty-Eight

Over in Myatts Fields South, inside Leandra's house, sits Thomas, Paro and Leandra. Thomas is gassing. 'Yeah, mi nah tell yuh man, mi bruck up di yute. Mash him up.'

Paro pulls on his spliff. 'True stories, rudeboy?' He blows out smoke.

Thomas sucks his teeth. 'Im lucky. Im nearly dead out deh. Di yute lucky seh im breddrin cum help.'

Paro laughs and looks at Leandra. 'So wot you saying, sis, you got two lick offa him as well?'

Leandra smiles, takes a puff on her stinking cigarette, then speaks in her British accent: 'Of course, little pussyhole.'

Thomas jumps up. He claps his hands and laughs then shouts, 'Yeah, man, mi girl nuh hitch.' Thomas looks at Leandra. 'Yuh nuh si seh shi buss di bwoy head wid a bahkkle. Mi tell yuh seh shi nuh hitch.'

Paro looks back at Leandra. 'Wot, you buss his head, rude...?'

Leandra nods, takes another puff, then replies, 'Sure bloody, and he was screaming like a bitch.'

Thomas and Paro laugh. Paro looks at Thomas. 'So rudeboy, wot you really saying? You gave him two jooks, rudeboy?'

Thomas's eyes narrows as he feels the pain from the headbutts Gunn gave him. 'Yeah, man, cool nuh, man. Mi gi im more dan two juk. Mi tell yuh seh im lucky.' Thomas sucks his teeth. 'Si next time mi ketch im. A dead im dead.'

Paro pulls on his spliff and blows out a thick cloud of smoke. 'You know once he's dead, rudeboy, da streets can be yours, rudeboy, d'you get me?'

Thomas bobs his head. 'Mi know, man. Mi agguh tek over dem street yah. A mi nayme Tammy Terrible.' Redy's face pops into Thomas's memory as he adds. 'Plus revenge a di sweetest ting next to pum-pum.'

Everyone in the room laughs as Thomas visualises killing Gunn.

Chapter Sixty-Nine

Gunn steps up to his front door and pushes his key into the keyhole. He is just arriving back home from the hospital where the doctor cleaned his wounds, plus bandaged him up and gave him some painkillers, which he does not intend to take. He told the hospital that he suffered his wounds from accidentally falling on some railings; he had no plans to report the real incident to the police. Gunn wasn't even going to go to the hospital but Cadija had begged him to go from the moment he got into her car after being stabbed.

John Wayne says to his boys, 'OK, lads, time for a debriefing.'

They stop their surveillance and head back to the Trident office to gather new information and drink lots of cups of coffee and tea.

Gunn steps into his door. He takes off his manbag and throws it on the banister, then climbs the stairs heading for the sitting room, followed by Abdullah and Driver. Gunn doesn't stay in the sitting room for two minutes when he makes his way to his bedroom, leaving Abdullah and Driver to take a seat. Just before getting to his bedroom the intercom bell rings. He answers it. 'Yeah, who's dis?'

'It's me, ak.'

Gunn knows who the voice belongs to and buzzes in Abdual-Hakim who is followed by Najash and Malo. Gunn waits till his Muslim brothers climb the stairs. Gunn says, 'As-salaam alaikum,' as his Muslim brothers reach him. They all say, 'Salaam, salaam, salaam.'

Gunn screws his face. 'Wot's salaam, acks? Give me my rights, salaam is for kuffars.'

Abdual-Hakim says, 'Astaghfirullah, brudder.' He embraces Gunn. 'As-salaam alalikum wa rahmatullahi wa barakatuh.' Najash and Malo repeat the greeting. Gunn leads the men into the sitting room.

More as-salaam alaikum echo from the men.

Abdual-Hakim looks at Gunn. 'You feeling better now, akhi?'

Gunn nods. 'Naam, alhamdulillah, mashallah.'

'So wot, you ready to burst dis yute's skin?'

Gunn smiles an evil smile. 'Not right now but soon. Inshallah.' The smile disappears. His eyes suggest a deep state of mind. Gunn had been thinking hard since he was stabbed, about the root cause of this violet chain of reactions. Gunn wishes he could break the link, but feels he can't.

Malo steps forward. He forms his hand into an imaginary gun. He points it towards the floor. 'Nah, his skin must get burst now. Today ak, dat Yardie must dead now. I swear down, I wanna burst him right now!'

Gunn looks at Malo and feels this is the reason why he can never break the link.

Abdullah rubs his nose and says, 'Hey, Malo, just cool, man. You're too greasy for a young yute, you know. Sometimes you must fall back and watch how da olders do it. Listen, don't worry, we're gonna burst dat Yardie soon.'

Malo shakes his head in frustration. He looks at Gunn with eyes that say, *I'm cold enough to become your right hand man.*

Chapter Seventy

Malo, Najash and Abdullah step out of Gunn's house. Abdullah is popping home to come back. Malo and Najash are on their way to Acre Lane to buy some food from their favorite Jamaican takeaway, Take Two.

Malo looks at Najash who is doing 60 mph towards Lambeth Town Hall. He shoots pass the Town Hall heading up to Myatts Fields.

Malo looks at him. 'Oi, I thought we were going up to Acre Lane?'

Without taking his eyes off the road, Najash says, 'Yeah we are, but I just gotta pick up something from my yard.'

'A'ight, cool.' Malo turns down the music. 'But you know wot doe?'

Najash makes no reply as he races up Brixton Road and passes the Police Station.

Malo says, 'You know we're looking like dickheads cos we haven't lick down dat Yardie yute, yet.'

Najash gives a quick nod. 'True stories, ak, cos it come in like Gunn don't wanna put in no more work anymore.'

Malo draws back snot into his nose. 'Init, for real, he must be tired. I know he's been putting in work for years but dis is da life he chose.' Malo looks out of the window and spots two of Gunn's younger Muslim brothers who both grew up off Acre Lane and are part of a new gang called ALC – Acre Lane Campaign. The guys walk out of Burton Road, a pathway that leads to Myatts Fields South, the south side of Myatts Fields North—Baghdad. They cross over Brixton main road.

'Oi, ak, stop da car, dere's Abdual-Rahim and Mustafa.'

Najash pulls the car over to the kerb, stopping outside the fried chicken takeaway that is five doors up from the off-licence where Gunn almost lost his life a day ago.

Malo winds down the window. 'Asalamu alaikum.'

'Salam,' replies Abdual-Rahim and Mustafa.

'Wot you...' Malo pauses as his sees Thomas and Leandra walking across Brixton Road from Burton Road and heading towards the Jamaican takeaway that is three shops away from the fried chicken shop.

Malo clicks his fingers. 'Hold on, ain't dat da Yardie yute dat shanked Gunn?'

Everyone looks at Thomas and Leandra who are about to enter the takeaway.

Najash's eyes widen. 'Don't lie, is dat him, gang?'

Malo replies, 'Yeah, ak, dat's him, akhi. He thinks he's some hothead.' Malo hits his fist into his palm. 'Oh shit, we should burst him now, aks.'

'How? Wot, have you got any sticks in da car?' asks Abdual-Rahim.

'Nah,' says Najash, as he thinks for a second. He looks at Abdual-Rahim. 'Oi, ak, you know where we keep da mash dem, init?' Abdual-Rahim doesn't reply. Najash continues: 'Listen, you and Mustafa run over dere now because I'm sure you'll get back in time before dey even get served.'

Abdual-Rahim and Mustafa are about to break out for the guns when Malo says, 'But Gunn said not now.'

Najash looks at Malo with a frown creasing the middle of his forehead. 'Bun dat, wot happen to all dat talk dat you wanted to lick him down today. Well, he's right here right now, gang.'

Malo again challenges him. 'Yeah, but out here is hot, aks. Brixton Road is flames, dere's ber cameras on da road, akhi.' Malo crooks his head up to look out of the window at the cameras.

Najash sucks his teeth in detest. 'Wot you talking about? Forget bout da cameras, man, we just tie up 'r hoodies over our face, init.' Najash hits Malo on the arm. 'So come man, bang-bang anywhere.'

Malo doesn't challenge.

Najash looks at Abdual-Rahim and Mustafa. 'You two hurry up and come back, man.'

Abdual-Rahim and Mustafa make their way over to Myatts Fields South in haste as Malo looks around at the Jamaican takeaway that Thomas is in, ordering what might be his last meal.

Chapter Seventy-One

'**G**i mi a large Oxtail wid Rice 'n' Peas,' says Thomas to the small slim woman behind the food counter.

'Yuh waan salad wid dat?' asks the small woman.

Thomas nods. 'Yeah, man an a Carrat Punch.'

Leandra is still looking at the menu board.

'Weh yuh waan?' asks Thomas.

'Um…let mi have…' Leandra looks at the small woman. 'A large Stew Chicken wid plain rice, no salad, jus coleslaw an a Irish Mash, please.'

The small woman finishes tapping the totals into the till. 'Dat agguh be fifteen pounds.'

Thomas pulls out a fist full of money and gives the woman a twenty as his name is called from behind.

'Waah gwaan Tammy Terrible? Bumbo,' says a young man who has never been to Jamaica, but when Rockne took over Brixton he was one of the English yutes who picked up the Jamaican accent and never lost it.

Thomas takes his change and spins around. 'Waah gwaan, my lawd?'

The English yute rubs his thumb onto Thomas's thumb. 'Tell mi nuh, mi hear seh yuh nearly kill ah yute out yah last night.'

Thomas kisses his teeth. 'Cool nuh, man. Yuh nuh si seh mi a original yawd man.' Thomas moves his arm from side to side in a sweeping motion. 'Nun a dem Muslim bwoy deah caan talk to mi now. Yuh nuh si seh mi nearly kill dem tap bwoy an dem cyaan duh nuttin bout it.' Thomas kisses his teeth again. 'Dem a fool, me soon tek ova di hole a Brixtan.'

The English yute laughs and hits his fist onto Thomas. 'Bloodclaat, talk di tings dem, shotta, yuh a gwaan wicked, hathead.'

'Mi naah tell yuh, man,' says Thomas. He scratches his head then continues to talk about his takeover as Malo and Najash continue to wait for Abdual-Rahim and Mustafa to return.

Chapter Seventy-Two

Najash looks out of the blacked-out window. 'Where da rass are those yutes, man?'

Malo looks in the rearview mirror at the takeaway, hoping that Thomas will not exit the shop yet. Thomas bought his food ten minutes ago, but is still inside gassing. Leandra is now begging him to leave the shop. She pulls on his arm. 'Cum nuh, babes, mek wi guh nuh.'

'A'rite, mi a cum,' says Thomas to Leandra as she lets go of his hand and walks to the shop exit. She steps out onto the pavement and spots Najash and Malo's car. She thinks nothing of it and turns back to the shop entrance and shouts: 'Cum nuh, man.'

Inside the car, Malo says, 'Shit, dey're leaving.'

Najash looks at Leandra, then back across the road. 'Oh, dere dey are.'

Malo looks across the road at Abdual-Rahim and Mustafa jogging to the car. As the young Muslim brothers get in the car Thomas steps out of the take-away and says, 'Likkle more,' to the English yute. Who replies, 'Nuh watch nuttin'.'

Abdual-Rahim gives the guns to Najash. Najash gives a gun to Malo.

'Take off da safety, it's already loaded.'

Malo takes off the safety, puts on his hood, ties it up over his face, and, with just his eyes exposed, pops the door. Najash holds his arm. 'Nah hold on, I think dey're coming dis way.'

Thomas and Leandra turn from the English yute, who makes his way back to the laundry from where he was selling his drugs. They walk towards the off-licence for something sweet that they can eat after their meal.

As they reach outside the sweetie shop, Malo and Najash burst out of the car and burst Thomas and Leandra's skin. The gunshots that burst Leandra's skin go through her leg and arm but leave her breathing. Unfortunately, Thomas is not so lucky; he ends up inside the shop, his blood splattered everywhere, along with the large Oxtail which is mixed in with Rice 'n' Peas.

Chapter Seventy-Three

Brixton is set alight once again with a symphony of sirens rushing to another murder scene. The man with the pretty flat nose is traveling on a bus from a wine bar up in the city two hours after the killing. His bus comes to a halt on Brixton Road at the Junction of Mostyn Road, a road that leads to Myatts Fields North.

'Damn,' he says to himself.

The driver says, 'The bus will be here for awhile. If you only have a few stops to go it's recommended you walk.'

The pretty flat nose man has got six stops to go. He gets off the bus and walks. He sees and hears other drivers who are stuck in the traffic jam asking what the cause of the hold up is. He knows it could only be one thing—another murder. He's just hoping it doesn't involve anyone he knows.

He gets closer to the sweetie shop, which has a small huddle of people outside it. His heart races as he sees a body on a stretcher with a white sheet over it being taken out of the shop. He stops just behind the huddle of people.

'Sorry, can everyone please cross over the road?' says a black elderly undercover policewoman who is wearing a bulletproof vest and holding a walkie-talkie.

The pretty flat nose man looks at her in astonishment because she looks like someone's grandma who spends their days in church sipping tea and eating biscuits.

'Excuse me, can everyone please cross over the road?' Repeats the elderly policewoman.

The pretty flat nose man is pulled out of his daze as an old hunchbacked white man with dusty grey hair says, 'Excuse me, what just happened here?'

The elderly policewoman takes a moment to answer. 'A black on black shooting. A murder.'

The man bobs his head as a smile reaches his face and eyes. The small huddle of people disburse from outside the shop.

The pretty flat nose man walks over to the other side of the road. He imagines his African ancestors saying to each other that they're not taking anymore liberties from their white captors, and then killing them as they arrive in Jamaica at a place now called Runaway Bay, then escaping to a place, which is now called Discovery Bay. He is sure they would be shocked to see these black men killing each other over things that don't equate to anywhere near the liberties that they had to endure from their white captors.

He shakes his head and thinks to himself: *I wish...I could some how transfer my thinking into the minds of these young black men so they can become what I've become—a creator of values. Because becoming a creator of values means they will discipline themselves to think, to gain control through the creation of values. And being able to create values will give them the power to break out of this elitist system which is the root cause that makes these young men think that they are worthless and can only achieve to be a gangster, drug dealer or killer.*

The pretty flat nose man closes his eyes and dwells: *How much longer will they kill each other until they realise their great self worth and what and who they're meant to be?*

He lowers his head, then walks towards his house as Thomas's dead body is transported to the morgue.

Chapter Seventy-Four

After the shooting, Najash and Malo clean themselves up then drive to Acre Lane where they buy food for everyone. Abdual-Rahim and Mustafa are given one of the guns that killed Thomas, then they depart.

As Thomas is being pushed into the freezer at the morgue, Malo and Najash arrive back at Gunn's house. Gunn already knows that they have killed Thomas. He is under stress because he had just planned not to retaliate against Thomas and take the opportunity to part from his Muslim brothers and leave behind the gang ting. His plan was to move to Egypt where he believes that he will become a devout Muslim and Allah will forgive him for his sins. That plan for now has gone down the drain because Gunn knows his name will be called for this murder and if anyone is going to retaliate they will be coming for him.

Gunn is gripping a silver magnum under a pillow. He locks eyes with Najash as his tall frame enters the room. He decides to give Najash a chance to explain his actions. 'Are you taking me for a joke, ak?'

Najash shrugs his shoulders and puts the bags of

food on the coffee table. 'Uh?'

Gunn screws his face. 'Wot did I say before you left out of here?'

Najash and Malo blankly stare back at Gunn.

'I said I will deal wid dat yute but not now.'

Najash raises his arms. 'Wot you talking about, ak?'

'Oi, bruv, don't take da piss out of me yeah, why da rass did you splash dat Yardie yute?'

Najash blinks and wants to say, 'Cos you're not repre-senting you dickhead, you're not putting in any work no more. You can't live off yesterday's fame.' But decides not to because Gunn exudes an aura that puts fear into the baddest of mens' hearts. Najash takes off his coat. 'Akhi, da long and short of it, yeah, we saw him on da ends going on like he's too bad for da world.' Najash sucks his teeth. 'And trust me, I just had a flash back to when those Yardies came over here in the nineties and had up Brixton.' Najash shakes his head. 'Real talks, I had to take him out, I hate Yardies, bruv.'

Gunn agrees with the last statement, regarding Jamaican "Yardie" gangsters and not the majority of hardworking decent Jamaicans, so makes no reply.

Najash raises his eyebrows. 'So wot, it's cool, yeah?'

Gunn releases his grip on the gun. He nods but plans to teach Najash a lesson for defying him twice and dragging him back into the world of beef that leads to hospital beds and cold morgues.

Everyone begins eating. Najash walks out of the room and creeps downstairs. He removes the gun that he used to kill Thomas, and puts it in Gunn's manbag that hangs on the banister.

Chapter Seventy-Five

Two hours after Najash and Malo came back from killing Thomas and buying food, they leave Gunn's house. They are being watched by John Wayne and his men... snap... snap... snap... snap goes the camera as the Muslim brothers get into their cars and drive off.

'See those little bastards? They are our future bread and butter,' says John Wayne.

Jack flicks his nose and says in a patronizing tone of voice. 'Yes, sir, you keep on telling us.'

John Wayne looks at Jack with stern eyes. 'Don't patronize me, son. You better take good heed to what I have been telling you. You are going to need it to repress your conscience when you finally see for yourself what is really inside Pandora's box.' John Wayne's blue eyes seem to turn a shade of green as he says, 'Listen, even if we used all of our resources and intelligence to arrest every last one of these slags, crime will always return.'

Jack and the other officer who had taken the pictures wait intently for more knowledge.

John Wayne wipes the corners of his mouth. 'Because there is another element that drives these bastards to do what they do. This is much bigger than their destructive mentality and ignorance. What drives them is a powerful force of nature, which is the need to be the silverback of the clan. All of these little bastards are struggling to be the silverback so that they can gain stimulation, dominance and leadership. So as long as those forces remain in man there will always be crime, wars and death.'

John Wayne turns on the car engine. His phone rings and he answers it. He makes no reply to the person on the other end. His eyes light up and he ends the call. 'Got him!' declares John Wayne. 'We have bloody got him now, lads. My informant says we will have all the evidence we need to link that scumbag to the killing that happened out on Brixton Road today.' John Wayne smiles. 'Tomorrow, at seven-hundred hours, we will be taking down a silverback.'

John Wayne pulls out of the tight parking space with the intention of returning tomorrow and kicking off Gunn's front door and arresting him for Thomas's murder.

PART THREE

PART THREE

Chapter Seventy-Six

The phone on Gunn's coffee table vibrates then rings. He gets up slowly from the settee and picks up the phone from the table. Gunn looks for a moment at his wifey's name lit on the screen. He then sits back in the settee and answers the call.

'Yeah, hello.'

'Babes, it's me.'

'Yeah, I know,' says Gunn apathetically, 'wot's goin' on?'

'Nothing. Are you feeling better, babes?'

Gunn twists in the chair. 'I'm cool, man. Dis ain't da first time I've been stabbed, you know.' Gunn's thoughts drift back to when he was fourteen and got stabbed seven times as he was ambushed by four gang members from Peckham, another ghetto area just a few miles away from Brixton.

'Yeah, I know, babes, but I'm worried about you,' says Cadija.

Gunn turns over the TV. 'Wot for? I'm cool, man.'

Cadija tuts. 'Listen, babes, I want you to come and stay at mines tonight.'

Gunn turns over the TV again. 'Why? I'm a'ight here, man.'

'Baby, please,' Cadija pleads. 'I just want you here with me tonight.'

Gunn throws down the TV remote on the settee. 'Listen, I'm not coming out my house tonight, man.'

'Why?' whines Cadija.

''Cos I've got to be somewhere in da morning, man, and plus you live too far.'

'But I can drop you there, babes,' Cadija says. Gunn remains quiet and Cadija adds, 'Listen, I'm going to come for you, yeah?'

Cadija hangs up the phone before Gunn can reply. Gunn grips his phone, shakes his head and looks at the TV with a pissed off look on his face which makes the right side of his top lip curl towards his nostril.

Chapter Seventy-Seven

About an hour later Cadija pulls up outside Gunn's house. Gunn lets her in and she enters wearing a long coat with nothing on except lingerie and high boots.

'I'm not coming to your yard, you know.'

Cadija sexily walks up to Gunn. 'Oh, babes, why are you behaving like this for? Please…' Cadija opens her coat revealing her red sexy lingerie. Her seductive perfume sweetens the air. Gunn gets an instant erection. He smiles then shakes his head. 'Wot's wrong wid you doe?'

Cadija gets on top of Gunn. 'Nothing,' she says as she kisses his neck. 'I just want to be with my man tonight.'

Gunn pulls his neck away. 'So why don't you just stay here?'

'I can't, babes, I got to be in my house all day tomorrow to wait for the electrician.'

'So how was you gonna drop me to where I need to go tomorrow?'

'What time do you need to get there?'

'From in da morning, init, I'm going to da Mosque. Inshallah.'

Cadija thinks for a moment. 'OK, if the electrician don't come by the time you want to go then you can take the car and drive yourself there.'

Gunn makes no comment.

Cadija kisses his neck. 'Yeah, babes? Is that all right, then?'

Gunn still makes no comment as he slips his hand down the back of Cadija's knickers. Cadija jumps off Gunn. 'No, wait until we get to my house.' Cadija pulls on Gunn's arm. 'Come then, babes.'

Gunn pulls back. 'Nah, just cool, just jam here, man."

Cadija swallows hard and falls into Gunn's lap. A frown appears on her face, as she knows she now has a fight to persuade Gunn to come to her house.

The Following Morning

Chapter Seventy-Eight

Gunn wakes up in a cold sweat at 6:50 A.M. He looks over at Cadija who is still sleeping from the two-hour work out that he gave her with his still-healing body.

Gunn closes his eyes and pulls his hand down his face, wiping the sweat. He flares his nostrils then opens his eyes. Quietly, he slips out of the bed and walks to the bathroom. Gunn stares into the bathroom mirror. He visualises himself being stabbed and he winces. He is then hit with the memory of the time he got shot in his chest. The moment the bullet pierced his skin the inside of his body felt like it was on fire. Gunn was repeatedly saying, *'I've gotta take off my clothes, I'm hot, I've gotta take off my clothes,'* to the people who came to help him on that freezing cold night. Gunn draws away from his memory and smiles. 'Allahu Akbar,' he says, proclaiming that God is the greatest. That Allah saved his life that night when he lost seven pints of blood on the pavement—if he had lost one more pint he would have been dead.

'Allahu Akbar,' repeats Gunn as he feels he must get

to Egypt and give his life fully over to Islam.

Gunn huffs. He turns from the mirror and heads for his manbag to read from his Koran. Gunn picks up his coat believing his manbag is underneath it. 'Rah, where's my bag?' he says to himself.

Gunn walks back into the bedroom. He turns on the light and looks around the room. He can't see the bag. 'Oi, C…C…'

Cadija turns. 'Yeah?' she says with sleep in her voice.

'Have you seen my bag?'

'Er?' says Cadija again as she rolls onto her front.

Gunn shouts, 'Oi wake up, man!'

Cadija opens her eyes. 'Yeah, what is it, baby?'

'Have you seen my bag?'

Cadija blinks. 'Your bag…? No, why?'

With agitation in his voice, Gunn says, ''Cos it's got my Koran in it. I need my Koran.'

Cadija shakes her head, then tuts. 'Is that it, you waked me up for that? It's only a book, you know.'

Gunn frowns, which hardly results in a wrinkle on his smooth skin. 'Oi, listen, mine how you're talking, you know. The Holy Koran is not just a book, it's God's Word. Astaghfirullah.' Gunn sucks his teeth. 'I should all give you a lick in your head, for dat.'

Cadija bites her bottom lip. 'OK, babes, I'm sorry. I didn't mean to say that. I'm sorry, I'm just tired.'

Gunn huffs as the frown disappears. 'Give me your car key.'

With distress in her face that makes her eyes turn to slits, Cadija says, 'Why?'

Gunn sucks his teeth. 'Just give me da bludclart key.'

Cadija doesn't argue although she knows the bag is not in the car. She dips into her handbag and pulls out the car key then throws it to Gunn. He catches it and makes his way to the car hoping to find his manbag.

Ten Minutes Later

Chapter Seventy-Nine

Armed police surround Gunn's home. John Wayne breaks down Gunn's front doors. He orders Gunn to come out with his hands up. After two more firm orders, John Wayne leads his men into Gunn's home.

Gunn's manbag swings on the banister as John Wayne and his officers rush inside and up the stairs.

The first room they enter, with guns aiming, is the sitting room.

John Wayne shouts, 'Clear.'

Everyone exits the room. John Wayne kicks open the kitchen door. The kitchen is spotless like it has never been used.

'Clear,' shouts John Wayne again.

Everyone leaves the kitchen and rushes down the hallway to Gunn's bedroom. John Wayne and his men reach outside the room. Without hesitation, John Wayne boots open the bedroom door getting ready to shout: 'Don't move, armed police.'

But remains quiet, as the room is empty. John Wayne puts his gun at ease and shouts, 'Clear.'

Jack looks at John Wayne.

'Bloody hell,' says John Wayne.

Jack clears his throat. 'Should we check the bathroom, Sir?' he says with a hint of sarcasm in his voice as he looks into the empty bathroom.

'Knock yourself out, Jack.' John Wayne brushes past Jack and shouts to all the officers in the house. 'OK, Ladies and Gents, let's tear this house apart.'

The officers' search for the next half hour until a female officer picks up Gunn's manbag and finds his Koran and the gun that killed Thomas.

'Sir, I've found something,' shouts the officer.

Chapter Eighty

The time is now 10:30 A.M. "Da Boy-Dem" left Gunn's house an hour and half ago after finding the murder weapon and two thousand pounds stuffed down a chair—which they will claim was only five hundred pounds.

Abdullah rolls up outside Gunn's house at 10:35 A.M. He gets out his car and approaches Gunn's door. He slows down at noticing the door looking out of shape. Abdullah looks to his right then his left then pushes open the broken door. Before he can step into the doorway, the person who lives downstairs opens their door.

'Hello,' says the small retired schoolteacher.

'Yeah—' Abdullah chin nods at Gunn's front door '—wot happened up dere?'

The retired schoolteacher steps back into her doorway. 'It was a raid… A police raid.'

Abdullah steps back out of the doorway. 'Yeah?'

'Do you know who lives up there?'

Abdullah turns his back on the schoolteacher. 'Nah, nah,' he says as he takes out his phone and heads back to his car. Abdullah presses send. He connects to Gunn's phone.

Gunn answers. Abdullah opens his car door. 'Assalamu alaikum.'

'Assalamu alaikum wa rahmatullah,' replies Gunn, as he is about to get into Cadija's car and head for the Mosque.

'Oi, akhi, where are you?'

Gunn opens the car door. 'I'm off da ends, init aks, why?'

Abdullah gets into his car and shuts the door. 'Akhi, listen, I'm outside your yard. You listening? Da Boy-Dem has kicked off your yard, ak.'

'Wot? Astaghfirullah,' says Gunn as he gets into the car and shuts the door.

Abdullah looks through his car window at Gunn's house. 'Yeah, real talks dey've kicked off your door, ak.'

Gunn starts the engine while thinking, *it was Allah's will for me to go to Cadija's yard. Mashallah.*

'A'ight, cool,' says Gunn, 'I'm gonna go Mosque den to my mum's yard. We'll link later. Inshallah.'

Abdullah starts his engine. 'Mashallah, akhi. Oi, you know where we're linking, yeah?'

'Naam, Plan B. Inshallah.'

Abdullah and Gunn both take off in their cars from the kerbs at the same time.

Later On That Evening

Chapter Eighty-One

Plan B is full of white people, as is usual on a Friday night. Plan B stands for Plan Brixton, a DJ wine bar on the Brixton Road, which used to be a fast food restaurant.

Downstairs in the manager's office, are Gunn, Abdullah and Abdual-Hakim. Abdullah looks at Gunn. 'Hey, ak, was dere anything for Da Boy-Dem to find in your yard?'

'Boy, wot could dey find…? All I had in dere was money.' Gunn kicks out his right leg. 'Alhamdulillah, it was a good thing I moved dem sticks out of dere da day before, Alhamdulillah.'

Abdual-Hakim and Abdullah says, 'Alhamdulillah!'

The door behind them opens, letting in a breeze that's carrying an odor of beer and sweat. In walks Plan B's events manager, a slim white man named Matt who is a friend of Abdual-Hakim's older brother. He walks past the guys. 'All right, lads?'

No one answers. Matt sits down and laughs nervously. 'OK, why I've asked you guys here tonight is because I've got some money to give you.'

Everyone's eyes light up. Matt continues, 'All you've got to do is call up this cunt—' Matt slides a piece of paper towards Gunn '—and tell him the debt that he owed Plan B is now owed to you.'

Gunn picks up the paper. 'Who's dis guy?'

Matt leans back in his chair. 'Oh, some cowboy promoter who didn't meet the bar spend and now owes five thousand pounds. But the important thing is he knows who you lot are and what you're capable of doing.'

Gunn folds the paper in his hand. 'Yeah, Alhamdulillah.'

Abdullah, with suspicion in his eyes, says, 'How much of da five bags do we get to keep?'

Matt coughs. He takes a second to work out that bags must be street slang for money. Slowly, he leans forward and says, 'Everything…everything is yours.' Matt clasps his hands together. 'But in return, I want you to get me some bulletproof vests.'

Gunn knows exactly where to get some bulletproof vests—Marlon, the brother of a police officer who supplies them to him.

'Is dat it?' asks Gunn.

'Yeah.'

Gunn, Abdullah and Abdual-Hakim rise from their seats and casually exit the office. They climb the stairs and vacate Plan B, leaving behind loud bassy dance music.

Two Days Later

Chapter Eighty-Two

The following day, after leaving Plan B, Gunn gives the cowboy promoter a call and tells him the deal. The cowboy promoter stutters from fear when he tells Gunn that he can only raise half of the money for the next day and the rest the following week. Gunn accepts his terms and is now making his way to the cowboy promoter's house, which is on Plato Road. A road that is off Acre Lane and named after the ancient Greek philosopher Plato whom laid the philosophical foundation that has encased the world in the system's destructive matrix for more than two thousand years.

The car that Gunn, Driver and Abdullah are in pulls out of Angell Town. Behind them in another car, carrying the guns, are Najash and Abdual-Hakim.

Behind Najash are John Wayne's boys: Jack and two other officers. Jack gets on his two-way radio. 'Hello, Sir, are you there? Over.'

'Yes, Jack, over,' replies John Wayne.

Jack looks at the car that Gunn is in, which is going towards the one-way system at the junction of Acre Lane and Coldharbour Lane. 'Yes Sir, the informant was right, we picked up the suspects from inside Angell Town. They are now traveling south down Brixton Road and if the informant is right, they'll be heading towards Acre Lane. Over.'

'OK, Jack, do not do anything until I get there. Over.'

With a pissed off look, Jack replies, 'OK, Sir. Over and out.'

Jack taps his two-way radio on the window. 'I really want to nick these scumbags, right now.' Jack bites his lip and shakes his head. 'Bloody hell, I want those filth off the streets so bad I cannot even sleep at night.'

Jack is still having nightmares about killing Devon Brown and believes by putting Gunn and his Muslim brothers behind bars he will make himself good with God again.

The officer driving says, 'Well, I am sure you will get some sleep tonight because I believe their goose is cooked.'

Jack smiles. He grips his two-way radio as his car cruises up Acre Lane behind Gunn and his Muslim brothers.

Chapter Eighty-Three

Driver pulls into Plato Road followed by Najash. Jack's car stops on Acre Lane. Driver stops his car two doors away from the cowboy promoter's house. Gunn and Abdullah get out of the car. Najash drives past Gunn and Abdullah as they reach the house and park at the bottom of the road.

Gunn knocks the door as Jack's car travels down the road and parks on the opposite side with Gunn in view.

Gunn steps back from the doorway as the door opens and lets out an aroma of African cooking. A short mixed-race man people call Mixey steps out.

Gunn jerks his head up and down. 'Wah gwan, bruv?'

Controlling his nerves, Mixey looks at Abdullah then back at Gunn and replies, 'Safe, man, you dun know. You safe?'

Gunn sniffs. 'Yeah, man. So wot you saying?'

Mixey grips his manbag. 'Yeah, um, I beg we deal with this inside my car.' Bleep-bleep, Mixey turns off his car alarm.

Mixey, Gunn and Abdullah open the car doors then get in.

'Yeah,' says Mixey, 'I already told Matt from Plan B that I was going to pay him.'

Gunn scratches his face. 'Dat's all long, cos you're not paying him you're paying me now.'

Mixey swallows hard. 'For real, but you know what though, bruv? I couldn't raise the whole of the two and half.'

With stern eyes that slightly close together, Gunn says, 'How much you got?'

Mixey dips into his manbag—'Boy, I only got one and a half, bruv'—and pulls out a bundle of money wrapped in cling film. 'Listen, I'll give you the rest next week this time, is that cool?'

Gunn looks deep into Mixey's eyes as if looking into his soul and giving him a deadly warning, then says very nonchalantly, mixed with a hint of firmness, 'Cool, next week. Inshallah'

Gunn is cool with next week because he recently found out no one will be retaliating Thomas's murder. Therefore, before any more beef can come his way he'll add the money he will get from Mixey to the thousands of other pounds he has stacked from all the past robberies and leave for Egypt for good.

Gunn and Abdullah jump out of the car leaving Mixey shaken, confused and scared from not knowing what to make of Gunn's cool approach in regards to accepting the rest of the payment next week. Mixey grips his steering wheel and watches as Gunn and Abdullah jump in their car and drive off.

Chapter Eighty-Four

Jack tells the officer to start the car. The officer, in haste, starts the car and pulls out of the parking space.

Jack contacts John Wayne on the radio. 'Chief, come in Chief. Over.'

'Yes, Jack, what's your location? Over.'

The officer swerves the car to the left into Solon Road. Jack grips the handle of his gun.

'We are heading northbound down Solon Road towards Sandmere Road, Sir. Over.'

'Jack, do not attempt to stop the suspects…'

Jack cuts in: 'I may have to if you are not here very soon. Over.'

'Negative, I reiterate, do not stop these suspects,' John Wayne orders. 'Stand down. Over.'

Jack says, 'Sir, with all due respect, I have had extensive armed training on how to stop and arrest hostile suspects. Over.'

John Wayne almost loses his voice as he says, 'What part of stand down do you not understand? Do not attempt to do the hard stop.' John Wayne's tone of voice lowers. 'This is a bloody order! Stand down!

OVER!'

Jack releases his grip on his gun. 'Understood, Sir, over and out.' He squints his eyes as he watches Driver spin his car into Sandmere Road heading towards Tintern Street.

Driver spots "Da Boy-Dem" behind him and decides to play with them. At the top of Sandmere Road he takes a right into Tintern Street and zooms to the top of the road. He takes a left into Santley Street then the second left into Medwin Street. This street will be the last street that Driver's car ever rolls down.

Chapter Eighty-Five

With distress in his voice, Jack says, 'Chief, come in Chief… What's your location? Over.'

He gets no reply.

'Chief,' he repeats, holding onto the dashboard as the officer spins the car in third gear into Medwin Street. 'These bastards have spotted us and I think they're playing cat and mouse games. Chief, come in Chief. Over.'

John Wayne answers Jack's distress call. 'Jack, where are you? Over.'

'On Medwin Street, sir…heading towards Ferndale Road, over.'

John Wayne doesn't answer back as Driver comes to the end of Medwin Street and is about to turn left into Ferndale Road when four loud gunshots ring out into the atmosphere. The bullets rip apart Driver's front right tyre.

He lets go of the gas pedal and skids into Ferndale Road—with his car out of control. Then his car is rammed from behind, making it shoot down the road a few yards and into a lamppost.

The doors of the car that did the ramming spring open and out jumps John Wayne and four of Trident's Special Armed Officers. They run to Driver's car and smash out the windows, shouting, 'Do not move, don't you fucking move! Show us your hands!'

Before Gunn or the others can move, the glass from the windows shatters over them. Gunn, Driver and Abdullah are dragged out of the smashed windows.

More police vehicles pull up on the scene. Officers with batons jump out. They attack the men. Gunn feels the first blow in the middle of his back and the officers saying, 'Get down, bloody get down.'

After the second blow, Gunn falls to the ground with more blows connecting as he makes contact with the concrete.

John Wayne steps on Gunn's back, pointing his service issue Glock SLP which is armed with thirty four rounds of ammunition, and says, 'You see this thing in my hand, I will fucking use it and then lie through my frigging teeth that you moved.'

Gunn spreads out his arms wider as his escape to Egypt penetrates his mind. 'A'ight Guv, cool,' he says.

John Wayne unclips his handcuffs as more police sirens scream towards him in the distance.

Chapter Eighty-Six

Six police vans arrive on the scene to pick up three unarmed men. Gunn gets thrown into a police van by himself while Abdullah and Driver share the back of another. "Da Boy-Dem" take the men to Brixton Police Station via Acre Lane which was once an old country lane back in medieval times.

Six police vans and two police cars with sirens blazing all zoom down the Lane to Brixton Police Station, employing a tactic to deter any attempt to ambush them and spring Gunn from their clutches.

John Wayne grips Gunn's handcuffed arms and pushes him into an interview room that smells of fresh paint. Gunn is forced to sit down.

'Wot, aren't you gonna take off dese handcuffs?'

John Wayne closes the door. 'Shut up. You act like an animal you get treated like an animal.'

Gunn looks to the ceiling. 'Astaghfirullah!' He shakes his head. 'Wot are you on? Man's got rights, you know.'

'What rights?' John Wayne grabs Gunn by the neck.

'You have no rights! Listen, I could kill you right now then lie my balls off and say you became out of control and while trying to restrain you, you suffered heart failure—maybe from the cocaine we found in your body.'

Gunn shakes out of John Wayne's grip and laughs, just revealing the top case of his teeth. 'Drop me out, Guv, I don't take crack. Astaghfirullah.'

John Wayne lets go of Gunn's neck. 'Well, maybe you do not have any cocaine in your body at the moment, but you will have once you are dead.'

Someone knocks on the interview room door.

Chapter Eighty-Seven

John Wayne opens the door.

'Hello,' says Gunn's solicitor. 'I am Mr. Raph Steele, from David Thomas Solicitors. I am here to represent my client—' Mr Steele indicates Gunn— 'Jerome Boor.'

'Come in,' says John Wayne as he takes off the hand-cuffs from Gunn's swollen wrist.

Mr Steele enters the room and pulls up a chair next to Gunn.

'The interview will start in a moment or two. I have just got to wait for my colleague.'

As John Wayne ends his sentence someone knocks on the door again.

'Come in.'

Jack enters the room.

'OK, we can start.'

John Wayne and Jack pull up chairs to the small green table.

'Now, do you understand the seriousness of the charge you have been arrested for?' asks John Wayne.

Gunn does not reply.

'Murder and Attempted Murder,' says John Wayne.

Gunn kisses his teeth. 'Murder on who? I didn't kill anyone.'

'Well, we found the murder weapon, a .45 Caliber in your house in a bag which we have photographs of you carrying.'

Gunn looks straight in John Wayne's eyes and says, 'Dat's not my gun, dat's not my bag and dat's not my house.'

Gunn had rented the house using false details.

John Wayne sniffs. 'Well, we have a witness that says that is where you live and we have photographs of you leaving the house carrying the same bag that had the murder weapon in it.' John Wayne clears his throat. 'So do not play silly bastards with me. We know it is your house, we know it is your bag and if you are claiming the gun is not yours then you better tell us whose it is.'

Gunn sniggers. 'I think you must be deaf, so I'll say it louder: I don't live dere, I don't own da bag, and I ain't no snitch.' Gunn switches his gaze back and fourth from John Wayne to Jack, and feels like saying, *Maybe you don't fully understand where I'm from and wot dat means. It means people can die by just accidentally stepping on somebody's foot. So young little yutes know dey have to get bad real quick and over-stand dis, every single one of dose yutes weren't born bad. Deir environment turned dem dat way. Like it turned me. I wasn't born a bad boy, I grew into dis, but I've gone so far I feel I can't turn back. I can now only go forward and obey da street code of silence.*

Gunn looks away from the offices, and then kisses his teeth.

John Wayne extends his arm over to the tape recorder. 'Charming,' he says as he starts the recorder. 'Interview commencing 16:45.' John Wayne looks at Gunn. 'Are you Mr Jerome Boor?'

Gunn looks at his solicitor; Mr Steele gives a firm nod. Gunn glares at John Wayne, and clears his throat. 'No comment.'

Tenement Yard and
Hospital Bedroom

Chapter Eighty-Eight

The next day releases bright cold sunshine down onto the streets of Brixton. Ten hours away on the little island of Jamaica the sun has just risen ready to beat down hot sunshine. The occupants in the tenement yard, that Thomas was raised in, is woken up by the ring of his sister's phone.

Thomas's sister looks at the screen. Butterflies hit her stomach as she stares at the foreign number.

'Allo,' she says with a crack in her voice.

'Allo,' replies a voice in the distance. 'Allo,' says the voice again this time not sounding so distant.

'Yes, a who dis?'

'Is dis, aam, Prinny?'

'Yes, dis is Prinny, a who dis?' replies Thomas's sister.

'Allo, Prinny, waah gwaan? Dis is Leandra. Memba mi fram round a di yawd?'

'Leandra...? Brown Leandra? Who deh inna Hingland?'

'Yeah, man, Prinny, a me.'

Prinny laughs. This will be her last laugh for quite a

while. 'Waah gwaan, Lee-Lee?'

Leandra stays silent for a moment. 'Prinny mi sorry…' she says as she swallows nervously. 'Mi have bad news…' Another pause. 'Ah Tamas…'

Prinny almost screams as she says, 'Ah weh wrong wid Tamas?'

The connection of the phones crackles as Leandra says, 'Im dead.'

'Waah?'

'Im dead… Tamas dead.'

Leandra gets no verbal reply, only a wailing cry is heard and then a dead dialing tone.

The Next Day

Chapter Eighty-Nine

It's late afternoon and outside is turning from day into night as John Wayne and Jack arrive at the hospital to see Leandra. They are there to get a witness statement of what happened to her on the night of the shooting.

Jack closes the door to Leandra's private hospital room. John Wayne extends his hand and gives her a firm handshake. 'Hi, I am DCI Wain.'

Jack shakes her hand too. 'And I am DC Mills.'

'Please lay back and be comfortable, Ms Watson,' says John Wayne. Leandra rests back into the bed.

John Wayne pulls out a tape recorder and presses record. 'This interview is being tape-recorded at Kings College Hospital, London. My name is DCI Wain and I am attached to Operation Trident. The other officer present is...'

Jack bends towards the tape recorder. 'DC Mills, also attached to Operation Trident.'

John Wayne looks at Leandra. 'And also present is Leandra Watson. The time is sixteen-oh-seven.'

John Wayne sips on the glass of water in front of

him. 'Obviously, Leandra, we were unable to get a statement from you when the incident first happened due to the seriousness of your injuries. But I hope you haven't forgotten too much of what happened to you on that night. So relax, speak freely, and I will get this wrapped up as soon as possible.'

'OK,' says Leandra.

John Wayne sips his water again. 'Can you just run through, to your recollection, what happened on the night of the shooting?'

With nervousness in her eyes, Leandra says, 'Well, um…I was walking down da road wid Thomas, init, and den dis black car pulls up beside us and out jump…' Leandra does a mental count in her head. 'Four men.'

'Did you recognize any of the men?' asks Jack.

'Yeah, yeah, I did, only one of dem, init.'

'And who was this?' enquires John Wayne with eagerness in his eyes.

'Some guy they call Gunn. He is the leader of that Muslim gang.'

The corners of John Wayne's mouth curve upwards. His eyes light up. 'So what exactly was Gunn's involvement?'

'Well, he was leading da other three men, init. He first said to Thomas, *so wot, it's you dey call Tommy Terrible?*' Leandra looks down at the table. 'Den Thomas didn't answer so Gunn said, *mash him.*' Leandra pauses. 'So one of da guys dat was wid Gunn pulls out a handgun from da pocket of his jacket. I screamed and Thomas shouted, *pussyclart!* and turns to run into da shop but den da guy shoots and blows a hole into Thomas's back.' Leandra picks up her glass of water and sips, then continues, 'And den as I ran towards Thomas a bullet hits me in my arm which throws me to da floor. Den I get another bullet in my leg and dat's all I can remember.' Leandra breaks down and cries. 'I'm sorry.'

John Wayne stops the tape recorder. 'No, it is OK. I think we will stop the interview here for an hour or two. But once you are fit to leave the hospital, which should be in a couple of days, you will have to attend the police station for the identity parade.'

'OK,' says Leandra as she wipes away her tears.

Back At The Police Station

Chapter Ninety

John Wayne brings Gunn from the cells. He informs him of the evidence that he received from Leandra.

When John Wayne had started the interview again with Leandra she told him about the night that her and Thomas attacked Gunn, which became Gunn's motive to kill Thomas. But her story was different. She told John Wayne that Gunn tried to chat her up in front of Thomas. Thomas then proceeded to tell Gunn that Leandra was his girlfriend. Gunn then replied, *'So wot?'* and punched Thomas in his face. Thomas punched him back, then began beating him up. Gunn tried to get away but couldn't until some guy who jumped out of a car helped him. Then this person fought with Thomas, so that's when Leandra joined in and hit the guy with a stick that she said she found on the floor. After she stopped hitting the guy he ran to his car with Gunn, but before they drove off Leandra said Gunn shouted at Thomas from the car window saying, *'Watch, I'm gonna get a hit out on you.'*

John Wayne throws Gunn into the interview room

handcuffed. 'Sit down.'

Gunn remains standing.

'Sit down!' shouts John Wayne as he pushes down on Gunn's shoulder, forcing him to sit.

'Now, listen,' says John Wayne as he takes a seat. 'I have a statement from the young lady you almost murdered.' John Wayne tugs Gunn to him. 'You should do yourself a favor now and make an admission of guilt.' John Wayne's face contorts with rage. 'Because you are going down! The only thing is how long you will go down for.'

Gunn closes his eyes, then opens them. 'Allahu Akbar.'

'Is that all you have to say?'

Gunn does not reply. John Wayne lets go of him, then opens the door. He shouts, 'June, can you bring in the video identification equipment, please?'

Moments later, June enters with the video digital camera and laptop.

'Stand up,' orders John Wayne.

Gunn doesn't move.

'I said stand up, you mug,' repeats John Wayne as he pulls Gunn up from the seat. John Wayne pushes Gunn up against the wall. 'OK, June, shoot him.'

June points the camera lens towards Gunn's face. 'Can you look into the camera, please?'

Gunn sucks his teeth. June huffs and circles around Gunn until she has captured every angle of his face.

Gunn is told to sit back down. John Wayne spins the laptop to Gunn and flicks through pictures of males. 'Pick eight of these faces that you want to be used in your video identification parade.'

Gunn glances at the laptop screen. He wonders, *why dis man is a racist? Why does he hate black people?* Gunn thinks, *dis man should love black people because his race came from da black man. If da black man didn't survive nature's harsh survival pressures, him and his race would not be here.* Gunn decides it would be pointless saying this. His mouth creases into a smile and he says, 'Go suck your dad, man.'

John Wayne's eyes seem to suggest that he is taken aback in thought. He then rolls them and says, 'OK, I guess I'll pick them for you.' John Wayne spins back the laptop.

A Couple
Days Later

Chapter Ninety-One

The video identification suite door opens. John Wayne, Jack, a female officer and Leandra enter with cups of hot beverages. Everyone sits down on comfy chairs facing a widescreen laptop. After Gunn had his picture taken and John Wayne picked eight other random males—all drug addicts who do ID parades to get money for drugs—it was Abdullah's turn, then Driver.

John Wayne opens up the laptop and inserts the CD, which contains Gunn's video identification parade.

'OK, Ms Watson, you have been asked here today to see if you can identify the persons whom were present at the time of the shooting.'

Leandra nods. 'OK,' she says then sips on her drink.

'I want to make it clear to you that one of the persons you saw may or may not be on the video film. Do you understand?'

'Yes,' replies Leandra as she looks from John Wayne to Jack and back.

'OK, I am going to show you the video film twice then ask you some questions. Do you understand?'

'Yeah, I understand.'

John Wayne starts the video parade showing Gunn in position five, the only position which June had manage to get him to look directly into the camera. The film is stopped after Leandra views it twice.

John Wayne clears his throat. 'Do you wish to view all or part of the film again?'

Leandra shakes her head. 'No—Gunn is number five.'

John Wayne plays number five again. Gunn's face appears.

Leandra points at the screen. 'Him, dat's him, he's da one dat gave da order to shoot me and Thomas.'

John Wayne takes his hand off the mouse and says, 'Are you sure?'

Leandra nods, but her eyes show a lack of assurance.

John Wayne says, 'So you are sure this is the man who ordered another man to shoot Thomas Patterson, and then this man shot you?'

Leandra nods again, but this time her eyes have hardened like steel. Making direct eye contact with John Wayne, she assuredly says, 'Yes, dat's him, Gunn, dat's him.' Tears spring from her eyes and tumble down her face. The policewoman comforts her.

John Wayne ejects the CD and puts in another that contains Driver and more drug addicts.

'Just like before, I am going to play the video twice, take your time and see if there is anyone on this video you recognize,' says John Wayne in a tender voice as he plays the video. After seeing the video of Driver and the other men twice, Leandra wipes her eyes saying she doesn't recognize anyone. John Wayne puts in another CD that contains Abdullah and more drug addicts. The last person to appear on the screen is Abdullah. Leandra points. 'Dat's him. Dat's da guy who killed Tommy and shot me.'

A smile draws across John Wayne's face. He has now got enough evidence to send Gunn and Abdullah to trial for murder and attempted murder.

Eight Months Later

Chapter Ninety-Two

The first day of Gunn and Abdullah's trial begins with the Crown Prosecutor's opening statement about the murder and attempted murder of Leandra and Thomas. At the end of the prosecutor's statement the jury have Gunn and Abdullah up in their minds as ruthless heartless killers. It gets no better when the Court adjourns for a break and the Prosecutor questions Leandra, which makes her break down into tears. But things are about to change as Leandra waits to be called back into the court to be crossed examined by the defense.

Leandra sits with Thomas's sister who has just arrived in England. She had saved her money for the past seven months, sometimes going without food, to get the plane trip so she could see her brother's murderers locked up for life.

Leandra squeezes her hand. 'Prinny, it's gonna be a'ight, dey aren't gonna get off.' Leandra shakes her head, then speaks in her Jamaican accent, 'Nuh a dem naah buss di case. A life dem a get.' Leandra nods and switches back to her British accent. 'Yeah, man. The LORD said an eye for an eye and a tooth for a tooth.'

Prinny closes her eyes and faintly nods. 'Tell mi again weh Tamas really duh fi mek dem bwoy deah kill im?'

Leandra's mouth twists as she flips back into her Jamaican accent. 'Mi a tell yuh, man, im neva duh nuttun.' Leandra changes her accent back to British. 'He was doing good, you get me?' She nods with reassuring eyes, then lies. 'He was going to Uni and working, cha man working hard, for real.' Leandra grips her face and sobs. 'And den just like dat dey kill him.' Leandra kisses her teeth and switches back to her Jamaican accent. 'All now mi cyaan believe it. When im drap a grung mi bawl fi im nuh dead.' Leandra starts bawling.

Prinny holds her in her arms. 'Hush, hush.' Prinny bites down on her lip. 'Nuh worry, dawg a guh nyam dem suppa.'

The door of the room is knocked on and a young black female police officer enters. 'It's time,' she says.

Leandra and Prinny are lead out of the victim support room and back into the court where Gunn and Abdullah are about to learn their fate.

Chapter Ninety-Three

The large door of London's principal criminal court, The Old Bailey, a court named after the road it is on, opens. Leandra, Prinny and their barrister walk into the courtroom that reeks of old wood and an assortment of body odor. They take their seats and the barrister defending Gunn and Abdullah calls Leandra back to the stand.

Leandra sits in the witness box waiting for the questions from the defense barrister.

The barrister pulls down on his black silk gown. 'Miss Watson,' he begins, 'you had claimed previously that the way you were able to identify the gunmen who killed Thomas Patterson and injured you was from the floor. You claim that as the men walked away they removed their hoods and this is when the opportunity arose for you to identify the men.'

Leandra nods. 'Yes, dat's true, I saw dem as I laid on da ground bleeding.'

The barrister lets go of his gown. 'And you identify these men as my clients.' The barrister glances over at Gunn and Abdullah handcuffed in the dock.

Leandra nods again. 'Yes.'

The barrister clears his throat. 'Well, I am going to suggest that you are a liar—because we have just recovered CCTV footage that puts my client—' the barrister points his pen at Abdullah '—Jeffery Andrews, in a different place at the time of the murder.'

Leandra raises her eyebrows. 'Is it?'

The barrister shouts for the exhibit to be brought into the court. A TV and video recorder are rolled in. The CCTV footage comes on the TV screen; it puts Abdullah, at the time of the murder, waiting to pay for his petrol after he had popped home from Gunn's house when Malo and Najash had gone to get the food.

Judge McCooey, a good honest judge, who came into the business not to assert arbitrary power over the lives of other people but to see that justice is always served, promptly bangs his gavel and releases Abdullah.

Cheers from Abdullah's family ring out as vexed faces from John Wayne and the prosecuting team exit the court.

The Last Day Of Trial

Chapter Ninety-Four

'**B**loody hell,' shouts John Wayne as he paces the floor of an office at the back of the court.

Jack looks at him. 'They are both going to get off, Chief.' Jack hits his fist into his palm. 'I know it, I just know it.'

John Wayne's eyes widen. 'No, they are not. I assure you the other one is not getting off.' John Wayne points and orders: 'Sarah, go and get the girl for me, please.'

The policewoman leaves the office and moments later returns with Leandra.

'Take a seat,' orders John Wayne with a tinge of vexation in his voice. Leandra sits down and looks up at John Wayne who takes a seat on the desk opposite her. 'Things seem to be going pear shaped.'

Leandra looks to the floor nervously. 'Yeah,' she replies.

Slowly, John Wayne says, 'Leandra, are you positively sure that as you laid on the ground Mr Boor pulled off his hood and that is when you saw his face?'

Leandra presses her lips together. 'Yeah, I'm sure. He pulled off his hood. I saw his face.' Leandra gives a quick flick of her head up and down. 'Definitely I saw his face.' She lowers her head and shakes it. 'And I swear I saw da face of the other one. I'm sure dat was him also.' Leandra looks back up at John Wayne. 'Can't we get any CCTV footage from Brixton Road dat will prove it was Gunn who ordered da shooting?'

John Wayne grips the table. 'No, the cameras were not working that night.' John Wayne gets up from the desk and walks to the other side. 'No, the only thing we can rely on is your testimony. So you have to be a hundred percent sure that you are not hiding any details that might be used to discredit your testimony.' John Wayne looks deep into Leandra's eyes. 'You are not hiding anything are you?'

Leandra slowly shakes her head. 'No,' she says even slower

'Good, because locking up this piece of scum rests entirely on you.'

Leandra doesn't reply as the court clerk announces to everyone in the office that court is back in session.

Chapter Ninety-Five

Gunn is lead from the dock into the witness box and swears on the Holy Koran. He is questioned by his defense barrister for over an hour. He is now being cross-examined by the prosecution.

The prosecuting barrister turns a page in her black folder and continues with her questioning. 'Mr Boor, are you a member or ever been a member of, reportedly, London's biggest gang, with over two thousand members. A gang called—' the barrister looks at the page '—The PDC, which stands for The Peel Dem Crew?'

Gunn scans his eyes over the jury members, the prosecuting barrister, and Judge McCooey. He looks straight ahead and again feels like opening his heart and saying, *'Da Peel Dem Crew, PDC, really stands for Poverty Driven Children, which means children trapped in poverty, driven to do crime. Do you really think we wanna do crime? And I'm not talking bout da kids who got everything dey asked deir mummy for. I'm talking bout da kids, like me, who had to eat corn-beef, rice and cabbage, or dey eat nufin'. Nah, we didn't wanna do crime but on da flip side we wanna be rich, so we don't have to eat corn-beef, rice and cabbage, but we don't know how to get rich legally and no one isn't showing us how to get rich. So of course we're gonna act on our ignorant ways and peel man, and da man-dem ain't gonna change until the system changes from educating us how to build and maintain their ting to building up and creating our own ting. Inshallah. Once dat day comes crime will vanish from da streets, Inshallah.'*

Gunn slowly shakes his head as he is hit with a realisation: *most of these people don't want crime off da streets, dis is big business for dem and I'm da cash cow.*

Gunn smiles, then looks back over at the jury. 'Yes, I was a part of da Peel Dem Crew.' He looks at the barrister. 'But wot does dat prove?'

The barrister taps her pen. 'It may just prove that during your gang affiliated days you built up a fearsome reputation that gave you enough power to order a man to kill and attempt to kill another person.'

Gunn looks at the jury. 'If I'm a man capable of ordering another man to kill for me, den don't you think I must be capable to get someone to come to court and lie for me?'

A lightbulb of logic comes on in the heads of the jurors. The barrister realises and says, 'That is true, Mr Boor, you have not called any witnesses to vouch for your whereabouts or lie for your whereabouts on the night of the incident. So what I suggest to you is this is your admission of guilt.'

Gunn looks back at the jury. 'No it is not, I've told da truth. I wasn't dere dat night and I didn't order no-one to kill anyone.'

'No further questions,' says the barrister.

Judge McCooey orders the court screw to take Gunn back down to the holding cells and adjourns the court.

Two Hours Later:
The Summing Up

Chapter Ninety-Six

The crown prosecution calls five witnesses: the owner of the shop where the shooting happened, a resident opposite the shop, two forensic scientists with PhD's and one police officer. None of them are able to supply any evidence against Gunn and the prosecution knows it.

The prosecuting barrister's eyes look weary as she stands up to address the jury.

'Ladies and Gentlemen of the jury,' she says, 'it is important that one sticks to the facts. Fact 1: irresponsible thugs who show no regard for any human life gunned down a young man and his girlfriend. Fact 2: the murder weapon was found at an address, which the police believe to be the accused. Fact 3: the accused admitted to being a part of a notorious Brixton gang who are reportedly responsible for at least eighty percent of the crime and gun crime on the streets of Brixton.' The barrister clears her lungs and lowers her tone of voice. 'So I urge you today to please stick to the facts when making your verdict because my verdict in this case is guilty on all counts. I thank you for listening.' The prosecuting barrister bows her head to Judge McCooey and says, 'My Lord,' then sits down.

The defensive barrister stands up and turns to the jury. 'Rightly so, Ladies and Gentlemen, we do need to stick to the facts and the facts are: there is no proof that the address the police claim to be my client's belongs to him, furthermore the murder weapon which was found did not have any fingerprints or forensic that belonged to my client. In addition to this, the non sequitur evidence presented before the court—such as my client once being affiliated with a juvenile street gang—in order to prove his guilt of murder and attempted murder, is ludicrous.' The defensive barrister gives his winning smile that shows up all his front teeth. 'I am sure you good people of the jury shall make the right verdict when you also consider that the complainant had already wrongly ID'd the actual gunman, and even though Mr Boor has no alibi, please remember, in his own words...' The barrister skims his gaze across the jury '...If he is a man capable of getting someone to kill for him, then he must be a man capable of getting someone to lie for him. Therefore there is only one true verdict and that is: not guilty.' The defensive barrister bows his head to the jury. 'Thank you.' He turns to Judge McCooey and bows his head. 'My Lord.'

Judge McCooey puts on his glasses as the defensive barrister sits down. Judge McCooey addresses the jury. 'Murder is the most tragic and destructive crime that can be committed but what is also tragic is if an innocent man is incarcerated for this crime.' Judge

McCooey picks up a bunch of papers and shuffles them. 'I am confident that you the jury have all the necessary information to make the right decision.'

Judge McCooey bangs his gavel and adjourns the court as the jury head to decide Gunn's destiny.

The Jury Returns

Chapter Ninety-Seven

A day has passed since the jury had been sent away to make their verdict against Gunn. The information, which they dwelled over, was: if Leandra ID'd the wrong person who actually did the shooting, then maybe she had wrongly ID'd the person who ordered the shooting, too. But nevertheless Gunn had no alibi and he had been part of a notorious gang who were involved in the gun crime culture.

The foreman finally gets the rest of the Jurors to come to a decision on Gunn's destiny and then informs the court that they are ready to reveal their verdict.

One by one the Jurors walk into the courtroom. Gunn looks deep into their eyes as if giving them a warning not to make the wrong decision.

The Jurors sit down. The courtroom falls quiet. Then from behind the judge's chair come two loud bangs that could wake the dead. The court clerk opens the door and leads Judge McCooey in, wearing his over-size black silk gown and white wig.

'All rise,' shouts the court clerk.

Judge McCooey clears his throat and sits down.

Everyone else follows suit. Gunn looks over at Judge McCooey then over at Leandra then looks away into space as he visualises himself on a beach in Egypt.

'Ladies and Gentlemen of the Jury,' bellows Judge McCooey, finally, as he puts on his glasses, 'do you have a verdict?'

The Foreman stands up. 'Yes, we do Your Honor.'

The atmosphere is as dense as the Universe itself, as Judge McCooey says, 'What say you, guilty or not guilty?'

The stillness in the court is like nightfall in the Nubian Desert as the foreman opens up the piece of paper. He skims his eyes over at Gunn whose expression exudes one that does not have a care in the world, as if he is not possibly about to be sent to jail for life.

The foreman looks down at the paper, then over at Judge McCooey and bellows...

Chapter Ninety-Eight

'**N**ot guilty!'

An uproar of celebration erupts inside the court from Gunn's family and friends. Thomas's sister and Leandra run out of the courtroom crying.

Judge McCooey takes off his glasses and bangs his gavel.

'ORDER, ORDER!' he shouts as the noise of the celebration rises and seems as if it might get out of control.

The celebration ceases and Judge McCooey looks at Gunn's family and friends crossly for a moment or two, and then says to the jury, 'Thank you for your service. You are excused.'

One by one, each juror rises and exits the court. Judge McCooey puts on his glasses. 'You are a very fortunate young man.' Judge McCooey looks intently at Gunn, and says with his mouth in a slight smile, 'You are discharged.' Judge McCooey takes back off his glasses then spreads open his arms. 'You are free to go.'

Gunn's visualization ceases for a moment as he looks at the court screw as if to say, *let me out then,* when Judge McCooey orders, 'Bailiff, please release Mr Boor.'

The court screw opens up the door that separates Gunn from the court. Out steps Gunn with relief in his eyes, a picture of an Egyptian beach in his mind and a smile on his face.

As he walks pasts his family and friends who are in the above public gallery, his white Muslim brother, Abdual-Hakim, reaches out with a clenched fist to give him a touch and says, 'Yes, ak, you buss case like I buss man's face.'

'Alhamdulillah,' replies Gunn as he touches his fist onto Abdual-Hakim's fist and heads for the exit.

Chapter Ninety-Nine

Outside the court there is media, police vans and crying people.

John Wayne and his men are in a huddle. With a croak in his voice, John Wayne says to Jack, 'All right, Jack, fair enough, we messed up.'

With disbelief in his eyes, Jack retorts, '*We* messed up?' He taps his chest. 'Excuse me, Chief, but I think you are bloody bang out of order for saying that.'

John Wayne grips the front of Jack's shirt. He jerks Jack towards him and says in a high whisper, 'Listen, you cocky bastard. We're a team. We have to stick together. If one cocks up we all cock up. Do you understand?'

Jack nods while saying, 'I just want to know where one draws the line because I believe the line was overstepped when we witnessed that scumbag murder someone in front of…' Jack pauses as Gunn appears on the steps of the Old Bailey with his family and Muslim brothers behind him.

Without looking at Jack, and not taking his eyes off Gunn, John Wayne says, 'Mark my words, filth like that will always be back to eat his breakfast.' John Wayne nods. 'It is just a matter of time. He will soon slip, people like him always do...'

Jack doesn't answer as Gunn descends the courts steps planning to go straight to the airport and onto the first plane to Egypt. He passes Thomas's sister who has her phone pressed against her ear. Her eyes narrows as Gunn comes closer into view. She reads his T-shirt that has the word **BRIXTON** printed on it in bold letters. She swallows the hatred she is feeling for Gunn and wishes she has a gun of her own so she can make Gunn disappear like how she feels he made her brother disappear.

The number she has been waiting for to pick up answers.

'Mommy,' she says with tears in her eyes. 'Di bwoy buss di case, di dutty bwoy get haf.'

An ear-piecing howl reverberates through the phone speaker as Prinny cries harder, and Gunn disappears into a black car and drives off into freedom.

Early Hours Of The Morning:
Kingston Jamaica

Chapter One Hundred

The ear-piecing howling that came through Prinny's phone as Gunn drove off into freedom continues in Thomas's tenement yard that is scented with ackee and salt fish plus fried plantain and dumpling.

Thomas's mother holds her "belly bottom" and bawls. 'Lawd Gad, dem kill mi wan son.' She shakes her head in disbelief. 'Lawd Gad dem kill mi son.' She holds her head. 'Mi wan, son, Lawd Gad. A wey dis pan mi.'

'A'rite Mavis, cum. Si dung,' says a large elderly lady who came from uptown Kingston to comfort Thomas's mother Mavis, who is her stepchild. The elderly woman leads Mavis to a chair. 'Cum sit. Nuh worry, cuz di same knife weh stick sheep a guh stick goat.'

Mavis sits down with her face in her palms and tears falling to the floor.

The elderly lady looks towards the front door and shouts for her husband: 'Oi, Da'son, whey yuh deh?'

Da'son walks into the house, the same Da'son that came to England from Jamaica in the 1940s.

Da'son, even though he's eighty-two years old hasn't shrunk much from his once six-foot-six frame. He's still looking strong and capable of taking on a whole bunch of Teddy Boys. Da'son had finally moved back to Jamaica in the late eighties after buying three homes in England then selling two of them and still collecting rent from the third.

Da'son walks up to Mavis who is his love child, which means he's Tommy's granddad, so that means Tommy was Natty-Nya's nephew, and Natty-Nya's granny, Da'son's mum, is first cousins to Gunn's great gran, therefore Tommy was linked to Gunn by their great grandmothers being first cousins.

Da'son takes hold of Mavis's hand and sits down on a chair. 'All right, Mavis,' he says in his now much improved English accent, which he always uses when talking to his daughter. Da'son squeezes her hand. 'Do not worry yourself. An ignorant soul can never vanish out of existence.'

Mavis doesn't register Da'son's words. She sniffs up her tears then says, 'But dem kill mi wan son, dem fi dead fi dis.'

Da'son caresses Mavis's hand and calmly says, 'That makes no sense, because it is our own we would be killing.' Da'son sucks his teeth and shakes his head. 'The person who they said killed Tommy is our family.'

Mavis looks up at Da'son with eyes that say explain further.

'Yeah. I found out that aunty Ma'pums—' this is the name that Da'son called his mum's cousin—Gunn's great gran, '—is this boy's great grandmother. I cannot

believe how we made something like this happen.'
Da'son looks towards the floor. 'We should have made
sure a long time ago that everyone knew of their family.' Da'son looks up from the floor. 'We should have
took more time to teach them who was the real enemy
and it is them they need to fight and not each other.'

Da'son shakes his head and lets go of Mavis's hand.
Da'son's wife huddles up next to her husband and
Mavis. She places her hands over their backs and bows
her head. Da'son and Mavis follow suit.

They all stay bowed for a moment and seem to be
praying for these violent days to change.

Von Mozar hopes you have enjoyed reading:

Little Jamaica

Waterbuck publishing invites you to
leave your comments on the website:
www.waterbuck.co.uk

Previous books by Von Mozar:

Ignorance Kills...
Sexfiend

New books to come by Von Mozar:

Mr Bling
Do You Love Me? (With Sugar Raye)
Brenda's Baby
Beautiful
Little Jamaica - The Windrush Years
Little Jamaica - The Brixton Massive Era
Little Jamaica - The 28s Years
Little Jamaica - The Yardie Years
Little Jamaica - The PDC Years
Little Jamaica - The Muslim Era
Jamaica's Paradise

VON MOZAR

SPECIAL PREVIEW

SEXFIEND

This excerpt from Sexfiend pulls the reader into Von Mozar's destructive and poor background, which saw him forever dreaming of happiness and riches.

Unexpectedly he is given a book that promises him once read he will become happy and rich! After eagerly reading the book and not becoming happy and rich he losses hope of ever being rich but believes he could still get happiness if only he could find again the girl he saw in a park that he was too scared to approach.

More than a year later he finds her but dramatically losses her to a cruel sexual twist of fate. Falling into a state of depression Mozar feels he will never find happiness until he re-reads the book and discovers what he needed to use to generate his inner happiness.

PROLOGUE

RUNDOWN HOUSING ESTATE

Chapter I

THE LARGE DOUBLE ROOM is quiet. Seven sleeping bodies fill it.

Eschewal, twelve years old, lays on a bed with his auntie, who is four years his senior, baby brother and sister. The bed opposite occupies his three older brothers.

The nudging signal comes to him. He knows what it means, tries to ignore it, but she won't let him. Her hot breath blows down his left ear as she speaks.

"Oi, you wanna do it?" she says in a whisper.

Eschewal wants to tell her no but she persists, with her big thighs.

"Oi, Eros are you sleeping?"

Eschewal pretends he is and lets out a moan, but she continues.

"Hey, Eros do you want to do it?"

He answers dumbly: "Mmmm, what did you say?"

"Do you want to do it?" she replies.

Eschewal dumbly persists. "What… Now?!"

"Yeah, come on, man, please," she pleads.

Butterflies begin to swirl in Eschewal's stomach.

Reluctantly he climbs on top and meets with his aunty's half-naked body. She pulls down his Y fronts then guides his penis into her vagina. He places his head onto her young firm breasts and begins bouncing up and down, her hot breath blows down his ear as she moans and groans.

Eschewal buries his face in the mattress as the sex becomes more intense. The next experience is new to him but not that new that he didn't know it was coming. His butt cheeks clench as he ejaculates.

They carry on pumping for a while longer. She squeals for a moment or two, then before Eschewal can slip off she pushes him off. Eschewal rolls onto his back then rolls over onto his front.

Slowly, the same sickening feeling he always feels after sexing his aunt runs through his bones and makes him feel sinful, filthy, even evil. In this moment he wishes he could rip his insides out and not be the person whom he is; not have to live in poverty, and experience the horror he experiences.

Eschewal wants to cry but holds the tears because the worst thing about the experience is when it begins and before it ends, it makes him feel beautiful inside. And this beauty is more powerful than the sickening after-effects.

Eschewal finally close his eyes, hoping this haunting was another one of those dreams.

EIGHT YEARS LATER

Chapter II

ESCHEWAL TOSSES AND TURNS then shoots open his eyes. He has sweat running down his face and his heart is racing. He grabs his penis, which is rock hard, then realises the haunting is one of those neurotic dreams he has from time to time.

Eschewal begins to panic as he finds himself handcuffed to a hospital bed. Earlier he had been knocked down as he tried to escape from "Da Boy-Dem".

He looks to his left and two other beds come into view. The one in the middle is empty but its sheets are ruffled. The one at the end is neatly made up. He looks towards the ceiling and closes his eyes.

Eschewal has had enough of the street life, had enough of being chased by "Da Boy-Dem". He has had enough of being locked up in cells and most of all he has had enough of feeling pain. Tears come to his eyes as nothing comes to his mind on how to escape the grime that he's been trapped in, since the days he started having sex with his aunty.

Eschewal whispers to himself: *"Why?"* Before he can repeat, *why me?* a flood of tears from the entire repressed pain, anger and ignorance roll down his face. As Eschewal bawls, he loses himself and slips into his own private world and all sounds from the past and the present are blocked out. While there Eschewal wishes someone could show him how to find happiness. All he really wants is to lead a good life that involves marriage, kids and a job.

Gently in the background, the sound of music and a powerful light voice shakes Eschewal out of his semi-consciousness.

"Do you want me to call someone, son?" repeats the voice.

Eschewal opens his eyes but doesn't answer. The voice continues to question: "What are all those tears for?"

Eschewal remains quiet. The voice continues: "I bet I can guess why you're crying. You wish you could have the nice things in life without experiencing any pain."

That sentence gets Eschewal's full attention. He wipes his tears and focuses on the old man's wrinkled face and strong youthful eyes, which reflect genuine honesty.

The old man stares at Eschewal before continuing. "What if I told you that the words in this book," the old man removes a medium size black book from under his pillow, "hold the key to make you happy, rich and powerful enough to never again feel pain. Would you believe me?"

Eschewal speaks for the first time: "I don't know, does it?"

"Yes it does, and much more, just as long as you read it and use the knowledge. But remember whatever you learn you don't need to believe, you need to accept."

Eschewal laughs lightly, holds his waist and screws his face from the pain as he sits up. "Listen, I don't read books!" he exclaims.

The old man nods his head. "I know you don't read. Most people where you come from don't either. That's why most experience a life of pain and hardship."

The old man rises slightly from the bed and extends the book towards Eschewal. "Take it, read the book."

Eschewal leaves the old man hanging, he is intrigued so he questions: "But why give me the book?"

The old man smiles and simply says: "I have finished with it, I no longer need it."

Eschewal extends his hand but is restricted by the handcuffs. The old man stretches closer and says: "Remember, the use of knowledge is power!" then drops the book into Eschewal's hand.

Suddenly a strange feeling comes over Eschewal, the old man continues talking but Eschewal doesn't hear, his thoughts are captivated by the book's title.

HOW TO CREATE YOUR DESTINY AND FOREVER LIVE LIFE WITH HAPPINESS & RICHES

Eschewal looks up towards the old man for an explanation of the title, but the old man has already left the room. This leaves Eschewal without a choice. He opens the book to the first page and begins reading.

Chapter III

ESCHEWAL READS THE FIRST line of the book.

You're the creator of your own destiny.

Surprise dons Eschewal's face. He licks his lips and continues reading.

For over 2000 years destructive-governments have blocked the immense power, which dwells within every human mind from unleashing.

Eschewal removes his eyes from the page and blinks towards the ceiling. He wonders what could be this immense power that dwells within. His heart is pounding. He takes a deep breath and continues reading.

That immense power is the full use of one's consciousness. What is consciousness? Consciousness is the ability to debate with oneself, make decisions and ultimately create new values. One can only create new values once one has learned how to unleash one's full consciousness.

Eschewal places the book on his chest and closes his eyes. He knows the next thing the book will tell him is how to unleash his consciousness, so hurriedly he continues.

GLOSSARY
JAMAICAN PATOIS

ADDA	Other
AF	Have
AGGUH	Going
AH	Am
ARMSHOUSE	Fight or aggro
BAD BREED	Bad or Unruly Child
BAD MIND	Having wicked thoughts
BAHKKLE	Bottle
BAWLING	Crying
BARE	Many
BELLY BOTTOM	The Stomach
BETS SOON BUST	Comeuppance
BLUDCLAAT	Cruse word
BOUT	About
BUMBOCLAAT	Cruse word
BUNING	Burning
BREDDRIN	Brethren - a close friend
BRUK	Break
BWOY	Boy
CAAH	Because
CYAAN	Can't
DAN	Don
DAWG	Dog
DAT	That
DEAH	Here
DEH	There
DEM	Them
DEN	Then
DI	The
DIS	This
DUH	Do
DUNG	Down
DUPES	Friend
DUTTY	Dirty
FAAH	For
FI	For/Must
FRAM	From

JAMAICAN PATOIS

GRUNG	Ground
GUH	Go
GAL	Girl
HATHEAD	Hothead
HAFFI	Have to
HIGH GRADE	The finest cannabis
HINGLAND	England
IDIAT	Idiot
INA	In
INYA	In here
JOHNCROW	Bad person
JU	You
KETCH	Catch
LACKKA	Just Like
LANDAN	London
LAWD	Lord
LEADDA	Leader
LIBATY	Liberty
MEK	Make
MEMBA	Remember
MI	Me
MON	Man
MUDDA	Mother
NAH	No
NAT	Not
NUHBADY	Nobody
NUH	Don't, Do, No
NUTTUN	Nothing
NYAM	Eat
PAN	On
PRAMISE	Promise
PUM-PUM	Vagina
RAH	An expression
RAHTID	An expression
RASS	An expression
RED-EYE	Jealousy

JAMAICAN PATOIS

SAH	Sir
SAAF	Soft
SCREW - ED	To stare with contempt
SE	See
SEEN	OK
SEH	Say
SHEGGIRE	Aggro
SHI	She
SHOTTAS	Gangster
SHUT	Shirt
SMADDY	Somebody
SUCKA BOLO	To give oral sex
SUH	So
TARK	Talk
TINGS	Things
TINK	Think
TUNG	Turn
UNNU	You
WAN	One
WAAN	Want
WAAH GWAAN	What is going on
WATA	Water
WEH	Where
WHEY	What
WI	We
WID	With
WUK	Work or Sex
YAH	Here
YAWD	House
YUH	You or Your
YUTE	Youth

UK STREET SLANG

B	Brother or Baby
BAGS	A thousand pounds
BEAST	Police
BER	Many
BITS	Town
BLUD	Friend or Mate
BLUDCLART	Curse word
BOPS	Walks
BOY-DEM	Police, Government,Etc
BRUDDER	Brother
BRUV	Brother
BUN	Too time or Gun shot
BURST	Shoot
CAT	Drug addict
CHIEF	Fool
CHOPS	Bracelt
COLD	Good
CRUBBING	Dancing
DA	The
DARK	Bad
DEIR	Their
DERE	There
DET	Pretty
DOE	Though
DEY	They
DOUGHNUT	Fool
DUN	Done
EAT	Rob
ENDS	Town
FAM (Family)	Friend
FAZE	Not Bothered/troubled
FIRE BUN	Disdain
FREE PAPER SOON BUN	Run out of luck
GOTHA	Got to
GREASY	Bad
JAKES	Police
JAM	Stay
KING	Friend or Mate
LAOW	Allow
LAOWIT	Allow That

UK STREET SLANG

LICK DOWN	Shoot
LICKED	Rob
MAN-DEM	Thugs
MASH	Gun
MASHING	Making
NUTTIN' NUFIN'	Nothing
OFFA	From
OLD SCHOOL	Known for many years
ONE POP	One nightstand
PACKING	Carrying a gun
PEEL	Rob
PEES	Money
PEPPER	Shot
PLUM	Fool
RADIE	Police
RAGGO	Audacious
RASSCLAAT	Curse word
REAL TALKS	The truth
ROCK	Fight
SHABBY	Audacious
SAFE	OK
SHANKING	Stabbing
SHOT/SHOTING	Drugs/Selling Drugs
SHOTTERS	Drug dealer
SPARRING	Hanging out
SPLASH	Shoot
SPUD	Touching fist
STAR	Friend or Mate
STICK AND SWEETS	Gun and Bullets
STICKY	Dangerous
STONES	Cocaine
STRAPPED	Carrying a gun
SUTUM	Something
TEK	Item
TER	An expression
TRUE STORIES	Home
WASTE CHICK/WASTE MAN	Loser, Bum
WID	With
WIFEY	Girlfriend
YARD	House

ENGLISH ARABIC

AKHI/AK	Brother
ALLAHU AKBAR	Allah is the Greatest
ALHAMDULILLAH	Praise to god
AS-SALAAM ALAIKUM	Peace be upon you
ASTAGHFIRULLAH	I ask Allah forgiveness
BARAKA ALLAH	May the blessings of Allah (be upon you)
BISMILLAHIR RAHMANIR RAHIM	In the name of Allah, the Most Beneficent, the Most Merciful
DEEN	Islamic way of life
HARAAM	Forbidden
INSHALLAH	If Allah wills
JAHILL	Wrong doing
KUFFAR	Unbeliever
MA'AL SALAAM	Peace out
MASHALLAH	Whatever Allah wants
NAAM	Yeah
SALAAM	Peace
SHAITAN	Devil
SUBAN ALLAH	Glory be to Allah
TAGILLAH	Fear Allah
WA ALAIKUMS SALAAM	And upon you is the peace
WA ALAIKUMS SALAAM WA RAHMATULLAH	May the peace and the Mercy of Allah be upon you